STORIES OF NORSE GODS AND HEROES

By Robert Buckley

BASED ON STORIES OF NORSE GODS AND HEROES BY ANNIE KLINGENSMITH

Copyright Terran Empire Publishing 2017

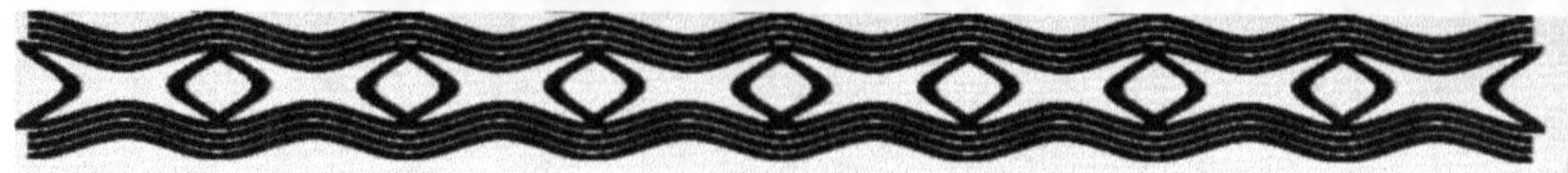

Published by Terran Empire Publishing

Terran Empire Publishing
1761 Hillside Court
Placerville, California 95667

First Printing, July 2017

Editor: Robert Buckley

Layout: Robert Buckley

Terran Empire Publishing Logo

by: Evan Rodda

ISBN: 978-0-9990108-2-2 (Print)

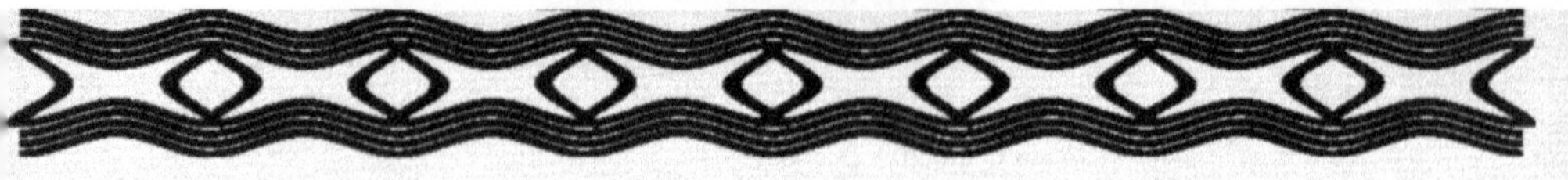

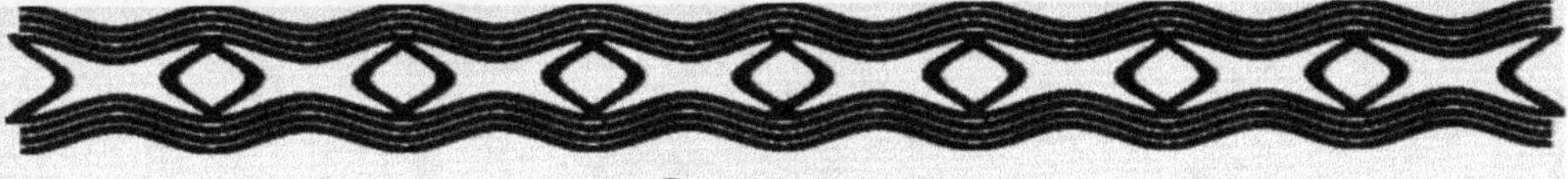

Contents

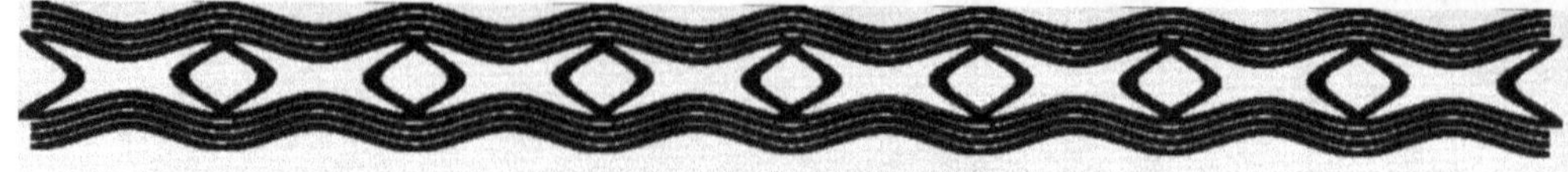

INTRODUCTION

Stories of Norse Gods and Heroes was originally written by Annie Klingensmith in 1894. It was published by A. Flanagan of Chicago, Illinois. It is a collection of Icelandic stories translated from the original Old Norse from the 8th through 13th centuries.

Poetry played an extremely important role in the world of the Norse. It is said that Odin, the leader of the Norse pantheon, brought poetry to Asgard through the Song Mead.

Old Norse poetry is characterized by alliteration, poetic vocabulary expanded by *heiti*, and the use of kennings. A kenning is a figure of speech that circles around a specific idea with multiple words. For example, Old Norse poets might replace the word 'sword' with 'wound-hoe'. One of the best sources of information about the poetic forms found in Old Norse is the *Prose Edda*, a collection that was written or compiled by Snorri Sturluson.

Typically, Old Norse poetry is split into two types – Eddaic poetry (sometimes known as Eddic poetry) and skaldic poetry.

Eddaic poetry consists of these characteristics:

- The author is always anonymous.

- The meter is simple, fornyrðislag, málaháttr or ljóðaháttr.

- The word order is usually relatively straightforward.

- Kennings are used sparingly and opaque ones are rare.

Skaldic poetry has the following characteristics:

- The author is usually known.

- The meter is ornate, usually dróttkvætt or a variation thereof.

- The syntax is ornate, with sentences commonly interwoven.

- Kennings are used frequently.

Special Note: Many of the names in the book have been anglicized in their original translation.

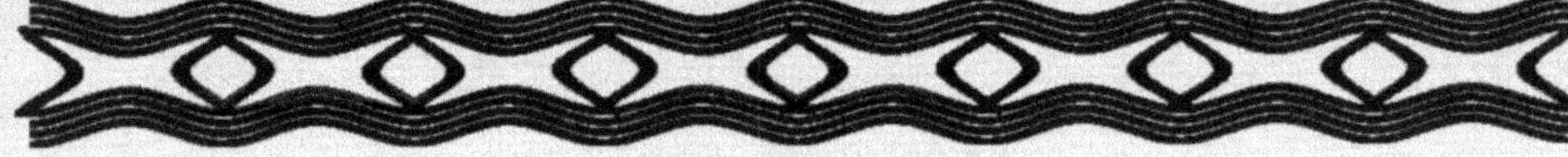

KEY WORDS

Norse - The term can mean the people of Norway or Scandinavia, especially the language they spoke during medieval times.

Asgard - One of the Nine Realms, Asgard is where Odin and the Gods of the Norse reside.

Mead - This alcoholic beverage is created by fermenting honey, water, and sometimes fruits, spices, and grains such as hops. Mead was produced in ancient times throughout Europe, Africa, and Asia.

Heiti - This is a synonym used in Old Norse poetry in place of the normal word for something. An example would be the use of the word jór or "steed" instead of prosaïc hestr or "horse".

***Prose Edda* -** Also known as the Younger Edda, or simply as Edda, it is a collection of Old Norse poetry that is widely assumed to have been written or compiled by the Icelandic scholar and historian Snorri Sturluson around the year 1220.

Fornyrðislag - This is a verse form that existed in runestones and Old Norse poetry. It means "past-words-law" or "way of ancient words".

Málaháttr - This is a form of poetic meter in Old Norse poetry, which can be described as "conversational style".

Ljóðaháttr - Meaning "song" or "ballad meter", a ljóðaháttr stanza typically contains six lines or two units of three lines each.

Dróttkvætt - This was a form of Old Norse skaldic poetry composed to glorify a chieftain's deeds or to lament his death. It consists of eight lines, divided into two half-stanzas of four lines each.

Anglicized - This is a term used to describe something that has been made English, or translated from another language to English, sometimes changing the spelling of the original word.

FRITHIOF

In the Northland, among the mountains, lived Hilding, a vassal of King Bele. With him lived Ingeborg, the daughter of the king, and Frithiof, the son of Thorsten Vikingsson. Thorsten Vikingsson was King Bele's best friend and bravest warrior.

The people of the Northland had many enemies who would come in ships. They burned the houses and the harvests, slew the men, and carried the women and children away as captives.

King Bele and Thorsten Vikingsson were always fighting battles with these invaders on the land or driving them across the sea to their own country. So Frithiof and Ingeborg were sent away into the mountains to live with old Hilding where they would be safe.

All day long, the two children wandered through the forest. Frithiof held the little Ingeborg's hand and led her along the rough paths.

As they lay on the ground close beside the tiny brook, they heard the soft, sweet notes of the water-nixie's wonderful music. In the waterfalls, the stromkarls sang and sometimes they could hear the hill-trolls underground praying to Odin to give them souls.

Sometimes they found beautiful grassy places where the fair white flower, called Balder's brow in memory of the gentle god, grew.

So the days passes quickly. Frithiof grew straight and strong and tall in the mountain air. No maiden was so fair as Ingeborg. Even Sif's magic golden hair was not more beautiful than Ingeborg's as it fell over her rosy cheeks and soft, white neck. So brave was Frithiof that he slew a bear and laid the great beast at Ingeborg's feet.

On winter evenings, they sat by the fire and heard the little elves of the hearthstone who teach the wind how to sing in the chimney.

While Ingeborg embroidered with gold and silver thread, Frithiof read noble sagas of the gods and their chosen heroes.

But King Bele and Thorsten Vikingsson grew old and feared they might die of old age and not enter Valhalla. So Frithiof and the king's two sons, Helge and Halfden, were called to the house of the king.

There stood two silver-haired heroes, King Bele and Thorsten Vikingsson, leaning upon their swords. Many words of wisdom they spoke to the young men who were to take their places.

On a day when the sea shone in the sunlight and the white-capped mountains glittered like gold, King Bele and Thorsten Vikingsson stood upon the deck of their dragon-ship and slew themselves with their swords, that they might enter Valhalla and feast with the gods.

Then Frithiof and the king's two sons buried the dragon-ship close by the waves as the dead heroes commanded.

Helge and Halfden became kings of the Northland and Frithiof went to his father's house. There, he found many treasures.

One was a sword with a hilt of beaten gold. On the blade were magic runes. In time of peace, the runes were dull, but in battle, they glowed like fire. No man might meet this sword in a fight and live.

Another treasure was a golden arm-ring. The ring had once been stolen by a pirate and he carried away to his own country. There, when he grew old, he had himself and his comrades buried alive with his dragon-ship in a great tomb.

King Bele and Thorsten Vikingsson had followed him and looked into the tomb. There, they saw the dragon-ship with the sails set for sailing and the spirit of the dead pirate on the deck. Thorsten Vikingsson entered and fought with the spirit, taking away the arm ring.

ELLIDA.

The greatest treasure of all was the dragon-ship Ellida. The prow was a dragon's head with golden jaws, and the stern a dragon's tail with silver scales.

The dragon's wings were the sails and the ship could sail so fast that the swiftest bird was left behind.

A long time before, one of Frithiof's ancestors had befriended a sea-god. As he came in to shore, he saw the wreck of a ship. Upon it had sat an old man with sea-green hair and a foam-white beard. The viking took the old man home, but at bedtime, he left and set sail on the wreck, saying he had a hundred miles to sail that night.

Before he went, he told the viking to look on the sea-shore next morning for a gift of thanks.

At dawn the next day, the viking stood upon the shore and looked seaward. There he beheld Ellida sailing straight toward land, not a man on board.

These three treasures had belonged to Frithiof's family longer than any man could remember, and they were famous throughout the land.

Frithiof made a banquet for Helge and Halfden and Ingeborg. As he sat at the table beside Ingeborg, they spoke together of the time when they were children. Almost they forgot that Frithiof was a man a full head taller than King Helge, and Ingeborg was no longer a little maiden.

When the feast was over and Ingeborg went, she seemed to take the sunshine with her. Frithiof longed so much for his old playmate that he went to King Helge and asked to have her for his wife.

But King Helge answered Frithiof in scorn and said his sister would be given to no man but a king.

Frithiof replied not a word, but drew his magic sword with the flaming runes upon the blade. With one blow, he cleft in twain King Helge's golden shield where it hung upon a tree. Then he turned and went to his own house.

After a time King Ring, the ruler of a country across the sea, sent messengers to ask for Ingeborg. The messengers brought gifts of gold, and with them came many skalds with golden harps.

But Helge and Halfden refused to send Ingeborg. Halfden sent a scornful message telling King Ring to come himself and ask.

When King Ring heard the message, he smote with his sword on his shield as it hung on a tree before the door. All his vassals were called together and they set out in their dragon-ships to make war on Helge

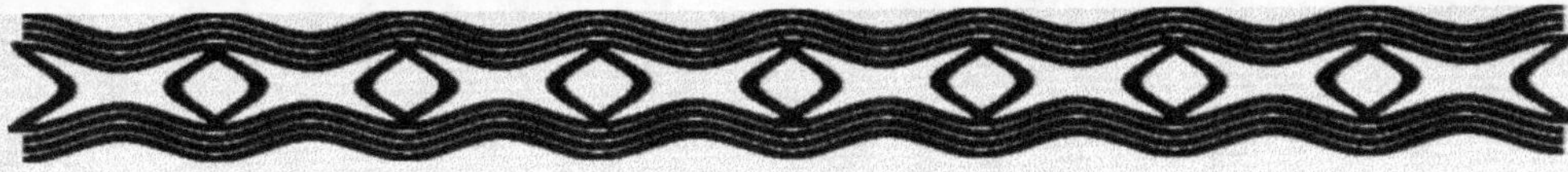

and Halfden.

The two kings sent old Hilding to ask Frithiof to help them against King Ring. But Frithiof replied they had dishonored him, and that he would not be their friend.

Ingeborg was sent to live in Balder's temple, so that she might be safe. There, Frithiof found her and begged her to go away with him, saying that he would defend her with his sword until he fell dead in battle. But Ingeborg would not go. Then Frithiof went to King Helge and offered to be his friend if he would allow Ingeborg to be his wife. A thousand warriors who heard him beat applause upon their shields with their swords.

But Helge would not listen. He said that if Frithiof wished to be his vassal he must go away to a distant land and collect tribute from Jarl Argantyr, who had refused to pay.

Frithiof hurried to Balder's temple and again begged Ingeborg to go away with him. The dragon-ship Ellida waited with her red sails set, but Ingeborg would not go.

She told Frithiof to be patient and go away and collect the tribute, as was his duty.

Then Frithiof gave her the golden arm-ring left for him by his father and went away alone in Ellida.

But King Helge stood upon the shore and prayed the storm fiends to send a tempest. Soon the wind began to blow, and Ellida leaped from wave to wave like a living thing.

Frithiof climbed upon a mast and looked out across the water. There he saw the storm fiends. One rode upon a whale and was like a white bear. The other was like an eagle.

Frithiof called to Ellida, and she turned and smote the whale so that it died, and the white bear was drowned. With his magic sword, Frithiof slew the eagle and the storm was ended.

Soon, they came in sight of the island where Jarl Argantyr lived. His house stood upon the shore and a watchman paced up and down the sands while Jarl Argantyr and his vassals feasted within.

When the watchmen called that a ship was landing, Jarl Argantyr looked out. He knew Ellida at once and saw that Frithiof stood upon the deck.

Atle, one of his vassals, seized his sword and shield and rushed down to the sea-shore. There, he and Frithiof fought upon the sand. At the first blow, both shields were cleft from top to bottom and Atle's sword was broken.

Frithiof threw down his sword and two warriors wrestled together. Soon Atle was overcome and lay upon the sand with Frithiof's knee upon his breast.

Then Frithiof said, "If I had my sword, you should feel its sharp edge and die." Atle replied that he would lie still while Frithiof went for his sword.

When Frithiof returned, he found Atle lying upon the ground awaiting death. But he though it a shame to kill so brave a man. So he gave Atle his hand, and they went into Jarl Argantyr's house together.

Jarl Argantyr sat in a silver chair high above the other. His robe was of purple trimmed with ermine. His golden armor hung on the wall behind him.

On the table before him stood a deer roasted whole. The deer's hoofs were gilded and raised as if to leap. Before the Jarl stood scalds and harpers, who sang of the deeds of heroes.

Jarl Argantyr welcomed Frithiof and asked his errand. When Frithiof told why he had come, the Jarl said he was not King Helge's vassal and he would not pay tribute unless King Helge collected it with his sword.

Frithiof stayed until spring. Then Jarl Argantyr gave him a purse of gold and he returned to his home. There, he found his house and his forest burned.

As he stood among the

 ruins, his falcon came and perched upon his shoulder. His dog leaped up

to lick his hand, and his snow-white war-horse came and touched his cheek gently with its soft lips.

Soon Hilding came and told him that King Ring had overcome King Helge and wasted the land.

To save his kingdom, King Helge had given Ingeborg to King Ring. At the wedding, King Helge took Frithiof's arm-ring from his sister and put it upon the statue of Balder.

Frithiof hurried to the temple. There he saw the priest with the king among them. In a moment he stood before Helge and dashed the purse of gold into his face. The king fell to the floor. Frithiof tore the arm-ring from the statue.

The statue fell into the fire on the alter, and in a moment the temple was burning.

Frithiof sailed away in Ellida once more. Helge followed him with ten ships, but the ships sank, for Frithiof's friends had bored them full of holes.

King Helge swam to the shore. He seized his bow to shoot an arrow at Frithiof, who stood upon the deck and laughed. Helge drew the bow with such strength that it snapped and Frithiof sailed away.

For three years, he sailed the seas, before he longed to live on land once more. As he sailed northward, he came in sight of King Ring's country.

It was just at Yuletide. King Ring sat in his hall feasting with his vassals. An old man wrapped in a bearskin entered softly and took a seat near the door.

The guests whispered together and looked at the old man with a smile. At that, he seized one of them and shook him until all were silent.

King Ring demanded his name. Then the stranger sprang from his seat and threw off the bearskin. There stood Frithiof dressed in velvet as blue as the sky and with a silver belt around his waist. His long, golden hair fell in waves over his broad shoulders.

Then King Ring swore by the hammer of Thor to overcome Frithiof in fight. But Frithiof only laughed and threw his sword upon the table with a clang. Every warrior at the board sprang up and swore to protect the noble Frithiof's life.

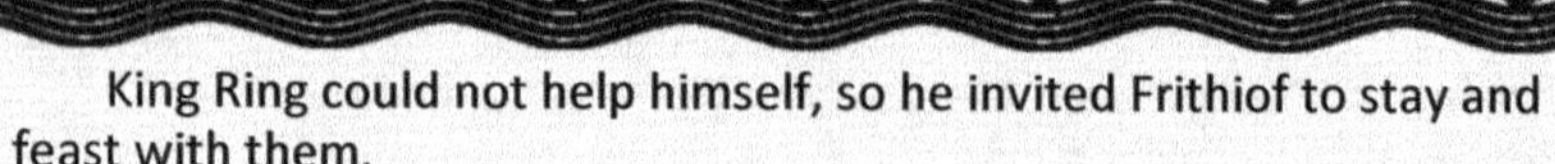

King Ring could not help himself, so he invited Frithiof to stay and feast with them.

Ingeborg brought him food with her own hands, and all night long they sang and feasted. So Frithiof stayed, and King Ring grew to love him as a son.

Soon King Ring was slain, and his little son became king of the land. All the vassals begged Frithiof to stay and rule the kingdom until the boy grew older.

But Frithiof went northward to his own land to make atonement for the burning of Balder's temple.

As he came near the place, he saw a phantom temple like the temple that had been burned. At the door stood Skuld, pointing to a shadowy temple far more beautiful than the old one.Frithiof knew that the gods meant him to build another temple. This he did. The new temple was so beautiful that it was like the halls of Valhalla. When it was finished, Frithiof entered and heard the songs of the white-robed valas, and his heart grew soft.

Then an old priest told him that the gods loved such gifts as he had given, but they loved better a forgiving spirit. And Frithiof heard with reverence the wise words of the aged man and forgave King Helge, who was now dead. Then he went to Halfden and offered his hand in friendship, and the young king welcomed him as a brother.

As they spoke together, Ingeborg entered. Frithiof asked once more to have her for his wife and King Halfden gave her gladly.

Frithiof built another house where his old one had stood, and Ingeborg came into it bringing the sunshine with her. Then Frithiof was as happy with his old playmate as he had been in the days when he took the little maiden by the hand and led her over the rough places.

KEY WORDS

STROMKARL: THESE WERE A RACE OF FEY BEINGS, ALSO KNOWN AS NIXIES OR WATER SPRITES. THEY WOULD SING BEWITCHING MUSIC, AND WERE SOMETIMES TREACHEROUS TO THOSE WHO CAME UPON THEM.

DRAGON-SHIP: THIS TERM FOR A NORSE LONGSHIP COMES FROM THE FRANKS, THE PEOPLE WHO RULED IN FRANCE DURING THE TIME OF THE VIKINGS.

VASSAL: THIS WAS A TERM USED TO IDENTIFY PEOPLE, MOSTLY LAND OWNERS, WHO OWED ALLEGIANCE TO PERSON OR COUNTRY.

A great army of men came into the Northland. They overcame all the warriors of the land, killed the king, and took possession of the kingdom.

The queen fled away through the mountains with her little son to the home of one of her old vassals.

Soon the soldiers came to find and kill the little prince. Again the queen fled, but her enemies always found her.

At last, she was afraid to stay in any part of her own country, so she sailed away to another land.

On the way, the ship was attacked by pirates. The little prince was taken and sold as a slave.

One day, the king of the country in which he was a slave saw him and bought him. He was given to the queen for a page.

The little Olaf was brave and handsome. The king had no son, so he made the little slave his son.

Olaf was taught to be courteous and truthful. He was trained to fight with sword and spear.

He could hunt, skate, swim, and walk on snow-shoes.

When he was at sea, he could run outside the ship on the oars. He could stand on the ship rail when the sea was the roughest.

He could use his sword with either hand and throw two spears at once.

When he was grown to be a man, the king gave him ships and an army so that he might go get back his kingdom.

At that same time, another king was leading a great army to conquer Olaf's kingdom.

Olaf went into the church to pray for a blessing on his journey. While he was praying, one of his warriors hurried in to tell him that the other king had set sail.

But Olaf would not go until he had finished his prayer. Then he set sail. He could see the ships far ahead.

Soon they came within sight of Olaf's kingdom. Then Olaf prayed the sea to roll over the land and make a shorter way for him.

The sea swept over the land and Olaf sailed on. As the water covered the ground, the hill trolls ran out and cursed him.

Olaf said, "Be turned into stones till I return." The trolls changed to pebbles and rolled down the hillsides into the valleys, where they are found even yet.

Olaf reached his kingdom first and the people received him gladly. They made him king and drove out the army that had come against the kingdom.

Olaf called his vassals to a great feast. They feasted all day long when suddenly, the door swung open. On the doorstep stood a tall man, wrapped in a blue cloak.

King Olaf called the stranger to sit beside him. All night long he told them wonderful tales of the gods and of heroes.

The night was almost over before they went to bed.

In the morning, the guest was gone. The doors were locked. The guard had seen no one.

Then the king and his men whispered, "It was Odin himself."

Away to the north lived a warlock called Rand the Strong. He worshipped the storm fiends, who often made storms to wreck ships for him.

When Olaf came into his kingdom, he was determined to punish Rand. He sailed away to the north. When it was dark, Olaf's ship crept softly up the bay.

Olaf and his men rushed in and overcame Rand the Strong before he was awake.

Then they sailed southward, taking his dragon-ship with them. Never had such a ship been seen in the kingdom.

But Olaf wanted a finer ship. He called Thorberg Skafting, the
 master-builder, and told him to build a dragon-ship twice as wide and

twice as long.

Thorberg Skafting whistled and sang for joy. His men, too, laughed and sang when they heard him.

All day long, they hammered and hewed. The noise sounded like music to Thorberg Skafting.

At last, the ship was finished, and Olaf and his warriors came to see it. When they came into the shipyard, the workmen stood staring. Some one had cut the sides of the ship from end to end.

The king's face grew red with anger and he vowed to kill the man who did the deed.

Thorberg Skafting smiled and said, "I am the man." Then he smoothed the sides of the ship until Olaf said she was more beautiful than before.

The ship was bright with gilding, and the figurehead was a golden dragon.

Olaf named her the Long Serpent. He sailed the sea in the Long Serpent many years. No king was strong enough to overcome him in battle.

But at last, three kings came against him at once. Olaf sailed with his fleet to meet them.

When they came in sight, he ordered his sails to be struck so that his ships could not sail away.

He lashed his ships three together and let them drift toward the enemy.

Then he ordered his warhorns to be played and the music sounded far out across the water.

King Olaf stood on the front of the ship. His shield and his armor were of gold and he carried his bow and arrows in his hand.

A sailor said, "The Long Serpent lies too far ahead. We will have too hard a fight."

Olaf drew his bow to shoot him, but the sailor said, "Shoot at the enemy. You need me."

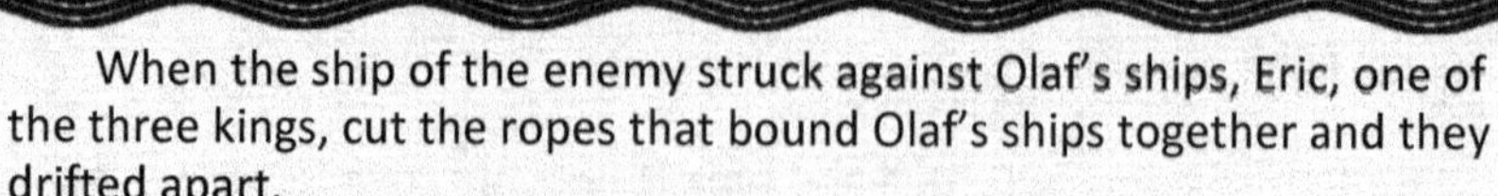

When the ship of the enemy struck against Olaf's ships, Eric, one of the three kings, cut the ropes that bound Olaf's ships together and they drifted apart.

Einar, one of Olaf's warriors, aimed all his arrows at King Eric. But Eric held his shield in front of him.

The arrows flew faster and faster. Eric called one of his men to shoot the brave bowman.

An arrow broke Einar's bow in his hands, but he only laughed.

Olaf said, "Take my bow and shoot Eric."

Einar drew the arrow over its head the first time he bent this bow.

Then he threw the bow down and sprang on board Eric's ship with his sword in his hands.

All day long, the battle raged until the decks were red and Olaf's ships were only wrecks. Then Eric's men boarded them.

Olaf stood on the deck with the spears flying about him.

As Eric's men rushed across the deck, Olaf's captain sprang to his side and held his shield in front of the king.

For a moment, the captain whispered in the king's ear.

Then the two men sprang over the side of the ship. Eric's men only saw the flash of their golden hair before they were gone and there was nothing but two shields floating on the water.

The people thought that Olaf stripped off his armor as he swam beneath the water, and that some time he would come again.

But he never came back, and the people called him St. Olaf.

SIEGFRIED WITH THE HORNY SKIN

In a great forest lived a blacksmith and with him lived a boy called Siegfried.

No one knew who Siegfried's father and mother were. One day, when the smith was returning from a journey, he had found a baby lying on a bed of leaves under a tree.

The baby smiled and reached out his little hands, and the smith carried him home. And very pleasant and bright the little boy made the lonely hut for many years, and the smith loved him as his own son.

One day, when Siegfried was grown to be a man, he went into the forest to hunt. There he found a dragon's trail and followed it until he lost himself in the wood.

As he wandered about, trying to find his way home, he met a dwarf who rode a coal-black horse and wore a glittering crown.

The dwarf told Siegfried that he was near the home of the dragon.

The dragon, he said, had carried away the beautiful Princess Kriemhild and held her captive.

Siegfried forced the dwarf to go with him to show the way. As they came to the entrance to the dragon's realm, they saw a giant whose duty it was to guard the gateway.

Siegfried fought with the giant and overcame him, forcing him to show the way to the castle. There, the giant sprang upon him and wounded him. But Siegfried threw the giant over a steep rock and killed him.

Then he entered the castle and found Kriemhild weeping. But the maiden dried her tears when she saw Siegfried's broad shoulders and brave face. She gave him a sword which the dragon kept hidden. This was the only sword in the world that the monster feared.

Just as they were ready to go, a roar was heard. The mountain trembled and the dragon appeared, breathing out fire and smoke.

Siegfried seized the sword and sprang at the monster. The dragon breathed out fire until the rocks were red hot.

After a long fight, the dragon's horny skin grew soft with the heat and the blows from the sword, and Siegfried hewed him to pieces.

Dipping his finger into the melted skin, Siegfried found that it grew horny and hard like the dragon.

Then he bathed himself in the melted skin so that no sword might cut him. But a leaf fell between his shoulders, and one spot was left where a sword might enter.

Within the mountain lived the dwarf Siegfried had met. With him lived his two brothers.

While Siegfried was fighting with the dragon, the dwarfs carried out their gold. They feared that the whole mountain would be melted.

Siegfried seized the treasure because he thought it had belonged to the dragon. This gold was called the Nibelung Hoard because it had belonged to old King Nibelung, the father of the three dwarfs.

Siegfried took Kriemhild back to her father's kingdom. There, he was welcomed by the king, and Kriemhild was given to him as his wife.

For many years, he remained there and became the greatest hero in the kingdom. The king's three sons became jealous of him, but they could not kill him because no sword could pierce his skin.

Kriemhild alone knew of the spot between his shoulders. She told the secret to Hagen, her brother's vassal, because she thought he was Siegfried's friend and begged him to shield her husband in battle.

Hagen told her to embroider a little cross on Siegfried's clothing over the spot, that he might better know how to protect him.

Then Hagen hurried to the three brothers with the tale. One of them ordered a great hunt and invited Siegfried.

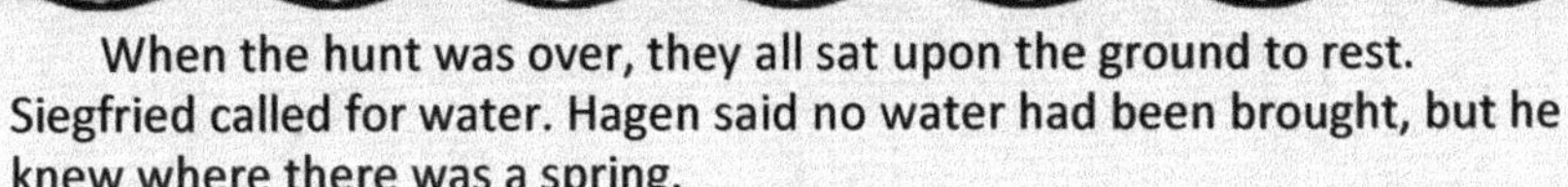

When the hunt was over, they all sat upon the ground to rest. Siegfried called for water. Hagen said no water had been brought, but he knew where there was a spring.

Then Siegfried asked to be directed to the spring. Hagen said, "I have heard that you are the swiftest runner in the land." Siegfried replied, "Let us all run a race to the spring."

The others laid aside their heavy armor. Siegfried kept his on, but reached the spring first.

As he stooped to drink, Hagen drove a spear through the little cross Kriemhild had sewn. Siegfried sprang up and seizing his shield, beat Hagen almost to death. Then Siegfried fell dead himself.

Kriemhild cared nothing for the gold after Siegfried's death. To prevent her from giving it to the poor, Hagen hid it in the Rhine, and no man ever saw it again.

SPECIAL NOTE

THE RHINE IS THE SECOND LONGEST RIVER IN CENTRAL AND WESTERN EUROPE AND FORMS PART OF THE BORDER BETWEEN SWITZERLAND, LIECHTENSTEIN, GERMANY AND FRANCE.

A long time ago, in a land near the ocean, there lived a king called Sigeband. He was a very rich and powerful king and had many knights in his army.

He often held tournaments so that his knights might show their skill in the use of sword, spear, and battle-ax.

Once, he held a tournament that lasted a week. Hagen, the king's little son who was some day to be king of the land, ran about among the horses and knights.

He looked at the sharp swords and shining armor. He heard the jingling of the golden spurs. He saw the gay plumes on the helmets and wished that he too, were a man.

He patted the shining coats of the war-horses and was never tired looking at them.

One day, he forgot to follow the men into the palace. There was a feast that day, and no one saw that the little boy had not come in.

The king and queen sat at the middle of the table. On either hand sat long rows of knights. All were jesting and laughing.

Suddenly, the windows were darkened as if a cloud had come over the sun. A roar that shook the palace sounded through the air.

Out rushed the knights with their swords in their hands. The king and queen followed them. They saw that a huge griffin was carrying away the little prince.

It was too late to do anything. The brave knights could only look after the little Hagen.

The king and queen went away sadly because they never expected to see their son again.

The griffin carried Hagen to an island far out in the ocean and gave him to its young ones for food.

As one of the young griffins hopped about in a tree, it dropped the little boy. He hid in the bushes and the griffins could not find him.

At night, he found a cave. In the cave there were three maidens who had been carried away by the griffin.

They were older than Hagen and took care of him until he was old enough to take care of them.

One day, while the griffins were away, Hagen went down to the sea-shore. There he found that a ship had been wrecked.

A dead knight lay upon the sand. Hagen took off the knight's armor and put it upon himself.

Just as he picked up the sword, he heard a roar and saw the old griffin coming.

But he struck the griffin so hard with the sword that it fell dead. Very soon, he slew the other griffins.

Then he and the maidens went down to the shore and watched all day for a ship. After a long time, a ship came for water.

At first the sailors were afraid to land. They thought the three maidens were mermaids because they were dressed in seaweed.

Hagen begged them to come ashore and showed them the armor and sword. Then they were not afraid.

The commander of the ship gave them beautiful clothes when he heard that their fathers were kings, but he was at war with Hagen's father, so he wished to keep the young man prisoner.

Hagen ordered the sailors to sail to his home. They refused, and Hagen threw thirty of them into the sea.

Then the commander let him have his own way.

When Hagen came into his father's palace, his mother knew him at once by the little mark on his neck.

King Sigeband made a great feast because his son had come back. The doors of the palace stood wide open so that any one who wished might come.

Soon Hagen was made knight. One of the girls who had been on the island became his wife.

When King Sigeband grew old and died, Hagen was king.

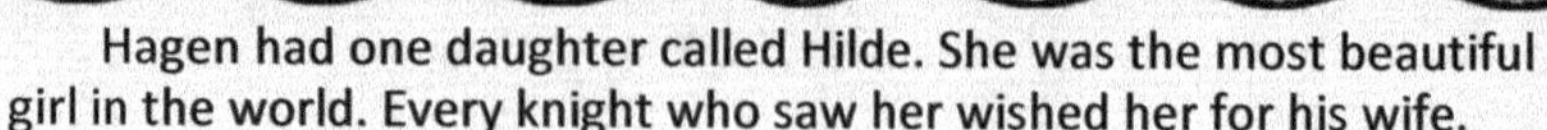

Hagen had one daughter called Hilde. She was the most beautiful girl in the world. Every knight who saw her wished her for his wife.

But Hagen did not think any one good enough.

Every one who came had to fight with Hagen. He was the strongest man in the land and he overcame them all.

Hetel, who was king of the Hegelings, heard of Hilde's beauty and wished her for his queen.

He called his vassals, Horant and Frut, from their homes and told them his wish. They told him to send for the wise old warrior, Wat of Sturmland.

When Wat found that Hetel was willing to have him risk his life in a fight with Hagen, he was angry and would not go.

By Frut's advice, they built a large ship. In the hold they hid armed men and sailed to Hagen's kingdom.

When they came to that country, they showed the costly good they had brought, and the people thought they were merchants.

They sent Hagen a war-horse as a gift. To the queen and the princess they sent silks and jewels.

The queen called them into the palace to thank them. There they saw the beautiful princess Hilde.

After that, they were permitted to stay in the palace.

One evening, Horant sang. So sweet was his voice that the night had passed before they knew it.

When the sun rose, the birds were quiet so they might hear him. The cattle left their pasture and came to the palace yard. The fish swam to the edge of the fountain.

The next day, Hilde called the young man to sing to her alone. He told her that King Hetel wished her for his wife.

Hilde said she would go if Horant promised to sing to her every day. Horant told her that King Hetel had twelve better singers than he was, and that the king could sing most sweetly of all.

In a short time, the knights were ready to go back to their own country.

Wat went to King Hagen to say good-bye. He asked the king to let Hilde on board the ship before they started. This the king allowed, because he never refused his daughter anything.

Everything was ready. As soon as Hilde was on board, they set sail.

Swiftly they sailed, but Hagen followed them as swiftly. The day after they landed Hagen's ships came in sight.

Hetel's army went down to the shore to meet them. Hagen was so angry that he sprang into the water and all his army followed him.

A fierce battle was fought. Both the kings were wounded. Then Hilde begged them to stop fighting and they became friends for her sake.

King Hetel had two children, a boy and girl. The boy was called Ortwein and the girl was Gudrun.

Gudrun was even more beautiful than her mother. King Hetel would not allow her to become the wife of any king in all that land. He thought no one was good enough for her.

Three kings, Siegfried of Moorland, Herwig of Seeland, and Hartmut of Normandy, came to ask for her. King Hetel refused them all.

Herwig returned to his home, but he came back to Hetel's kingdom with three thousand knights. A battle was fought by the castle gate. Hetel and Herwig fought hand to hand.

Gudrun saw the fight from her window. She ran out and begged the two kings not to kill each other.

For her sake, they became friends. Hetel promised to give Gudrun to Herwig.

As soon as Siegfried of Moorland heard of this, he gathered an army and went to Herwig's kingdom.

When Herwig could fight no longer, he sent to Hetel for help.

King Hetel went with his army and left only a few knights to guard the castle.

Hartmut of Normandy heard of this and came to Hetel's kingdom with a great army.

They captured Gudrun and carried her to Normandy with sixty of her maidens. Hilde sent word to Hetel. Very soon, he set sail to Normandy with his warriors.

Hartmut's army came down to meet them. A battle was fought on the sea-shore. So many men were slain that the waves were red with blood.

At last, Hetel was killed. The Hegelings went back to their own land sadly and left Gudrun in Normandy.

The knights went to their homes, but they did not forget that their princess had been carried away and their king killed.

Gudrun lived in the castle with Hartmut's mother, but she would not be Hartmut's wife.

After a time, Hartmut's mother grew angry and did not treat her as a princess.

Gudrun was made to do work like a servant. All the maidens who were taken with her were set to spinning flax and weaving cloth.

Gudrun swept the floors and made the fires. For thirteen years she did this work, but she would not be Hartmut's wife.

By that time, the boys in Hetel's kingdom had grown to be men. Wat of Sturmland led another army against King Hartmut.

Gudrun was down at the sea-shore washing clothes. As she worked, a beautiful bird swam to her. The bird sang of the great army that was coming to take her home.

When Gudrun went to the castle that night, the queen scolded her because the work was not all done.

The next morning, the ground was white with snow, but the queen sent Gudrun to the sea-shore to finish the washing.

Soon, she saw her brother and Herwig coming in a boat. The two men did not know her.

They were surprised to see so beautiful a maiden doing such work.

They asked her name and who dared treat her so. She answered that she was one of the maidens King Hartmut had carried away from the land of the Hegelings.

At this, the young men's eyes filled with tears to see a maiden of their own land standing barefoot in the snow.

When Gudrun saw the tears in their eyes, she told them who she really was.

Herwig wanted to take her away at once, but Ortwein would not let him.

He told Gudrun to go back to the castle and wait till they came with the army.

Gudrun threw the clothes into the sea. The queen saw her coming back without them, and sent a servant to whip her with a rod. But Gudrun said she was ready to be Hartmut's wife.

Then beautiful dresses were given to Gudrun and her maidens.

Hartmut sent his best knights away to ask people to come to the wedding.

Herwig and Ortwein went back to the army and told what they had seen. The Hegelings were so angry that they would not wait for daylight, but set off at once.

Early in the morning, Gudrun looked out and saw the sun shining on the armor just outside the castle-wall.

Soon the Norman knights were ready. They rode out with Hartmut and his father at the head.

Then old Wat of Sturmland blew his bugle so loud that it was heard for thirty miles around and the battle began.

Hartmut's father was slain. Old Wat cut his way through the knights to Hartmut. Hartmut fought for his life, but old Wat was the stronger.

Hartmut's sister, who had always been kind to Gudrun, looked out and saw that her brother would be killed.

She ran to Gudrun and begged her to save his life. Gudrun called Herwig to ask Wat to spare spare Hartmut's life.

Wat struck Herwig for asking, but he stopped fighting and took Hartmut prisoner.

The queen threw herself at Gudrun's feet and begged to be saved from Wat, but Wat cut her head off with his sword.

When Gudrun reached home, her mother was standing on the shore waiting for her. Soon she became Herwig's wife.

The queen sent Hartmut back to his own land. But his sister, who had always been kind to Gudrun, stayed in the land of the Hegelings.

ANDVARE'S GOLDEN RING

Once, Odin and Loke set out to explore the whole world. As they traveled, they came to a stream by which sat an otter eating a fish. Loke threw a stone and killed the otter.

Taking the otter and the fish, they went on until they came to a farmhouse. There, they asked to stay until morning. They showed the fish and the otter and said they would need no other food.

The farmer saw that Loke had killed his son, who often changed himself into an otter when he wanted to fish. He said nothing about it, but went out and told his other two sons, Regin and Fafner.

When the skin had been taken off the otter, the two sons came in. They and their father overcame the gods and bound them.

Odin offered to pay a ransom. The farmer demanded enough gold to fill the otter skin and cover it.

So Odin sent Loke to the dwarf Andvare, who was the richest of all dwarfs. He was also the wariest of all dwarfs. He changed himself into a fish and hid in the water.

But Loke borrowed a net from Ran, the sea-god's wife, and caught him.

When Andvare found that he could not escape, he gave up all of his gold but for one little ring. This he tried to hide under his arm. Loke took it away from him. The dwarf begged to have it given back. He said if he had the ring, he could make more gold; but, without it, he could do nothing.

When Loke would not let him have the ring, he cursed the gold and said it would always bring trouble to its owner.

Loke carried the gold to Odin. Odin filled the otter skin and covered it, but kept the ring. When the farmer looked, he found one hair that was not covered. Odin put the ring upon the hair and the farmer unbound him.

As soon as the gods were gone, the sons demanded some of the gold. The father refused to divide it and Fafner killed him with a sword while he slept.

SIGURD THE VOLSUNG

One Yuletide, King Volsung entertained his friends and vassals. All down the great hall burned roaring fires.

King Volsung sat in the high-seat with his guests on either hand. In the middle of the hall grew a large tree, the foliage of which covered the roof. This was called Odin's tree.

As the ale horns passed around, and the hall resounded with the laughter of the warriors, a tall, old mad strode in with a sword in his hand.

With one blow, he drove the sword into the root-tree up to the hilt. Then he exclaimed, "He who draws out the sword shall have it as a gift from me, and he will find that he has never wielded a better sword."

With that, he strode out, and no man dared ask his name or whither he went. But the guests whispered that it was Odin himself.

All tried to draw out the sword, but it was immovable.

When Sigmund, King Volsung's son, touched the sword, it was so loose that he drew it out with no effort.

After many years, Sigmund was slain in battle and the sword was broken. But the pieces were kept by Sigmund's son, who was called Sigurd the Volsung.

Sigurd was the bravest and strongest man in the world.

His eyes were so keen that few men dared gaze at him. His hair was golden and hung down over his shoulders, which were as broad as two men's shoulders.

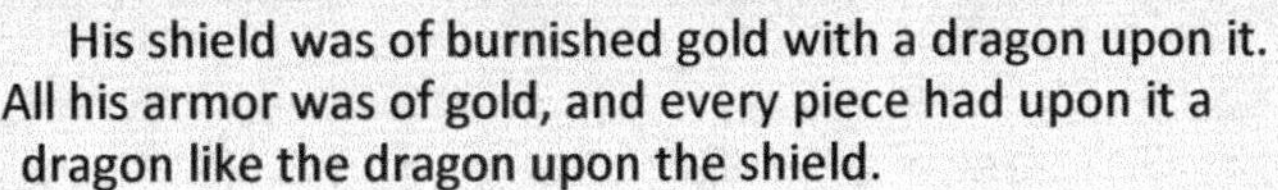

His shield was of burnished gold with a dragon upon it. All his armor was of gold, and every piece had upon it a dragon like the dragon upon the shield.

When Fafner went away with the gold that had been given by Odin for the death of the otter, he changed himself into a great dragon and lay on Gnita-Heath guarding the treasure.

Regin knew that he was not strong enough to kill the dragon, so he made a long journey to the land of a wise king to ask his advice. The wise king sent him to Sigurd the Volsung.

Regin told the Volsung of the hoard and Sigurd vowed to kill the dragon.

From Odin he received the good horse Gran and only needed a sword sharp and strong enough to pierce the dragon's horny skin.

Regin made a sword, but when Sigurd struck it upon the anvil, it broke. Regin made another sword and this Sigurd also broke.

Of the pieces of the old sword which Odin had given his father, Sigurd bade Regin make a new sword. When the sword was finished Sigurd cleft the anvil from top to bottom with it.

Then he went to a river and held the sword in the water. A piece of wool floated against it and was cut in twain.

Sigurd mounted Gran and, taking the wonderful sword, rode to Gnita-Heath where lay the dragon.

When Fafner heard him coming, he tried to creep away into the water, but Sigurd lay in the hollow in the ground and pierced him with the sword as he passed over.

Then Regin came and refused to share the gold with Sigurd as he had promised. When Sigurd demanded his share, Regin spoke smoothly, but in his heart he meant to kill him.

Regin bade the Volsung roast the dragon's heart for him. While Sigurd was roasting the heart he burned his fingers. Putting them into his mouth, some of the dragon's blood touched his tongue. At once he understood the songs of birds. "Regin means to kill you," sang the birds in the tree-tops. "Cut off his head and eat the dragon's heart yourself."

Then Sigurd killed Regin and ate the heart. Immediately, he overheard two eagles talking together.

They spoke of a castle on a mountain-top surrounded by blazing flames.

Within the castle slept a maiden whom Odin had pricked with a magic sleep thorn. "No horse but Gran" they said, "will go through the fire wall, and no man but Sigurd is allowed to wake the maiden."

Sigurd followed the dragon's track until he came to its den. There, he found the treasure in the chest. He put the chest on Gran's back, but Gran would not move until Sigurd mounted him.

Sigurd rode until he came to a mountain. At the top was a flickering light as of fire, and the flames shone upon the sky.

As Sigurd rode through the flame wall, he saw the castle. He went into the castle, and there lay an armed knight, asleep. When he took off the helmet, he saw that the knight was a woman. Then, with his sword, he cut off the maiden's armor.

She awoke and said, "Who is this that dares to wake me from the magic sleep?"

Sigurd told his name and the maiden said she was Brynhilda. Sigurd stayed three days. When he left, he gave Brynhilda Andvare's golden ring and a promise to return for her not knowing there was a curse upon the ring.

Then he traveled southward with the treasure to the realm of the king called Guike. The king had a beautiful daughter whose name was Gudrun.

When the queen saw Sigurd, she was pleased with his beauty and strength and wished him to marry Gudrun.

One night, when the warriors were feasting, she gave him a cup of magic drink which made him forget Brynhilda. Soon, he married Gudrun and no longer remembered that he had ever seen Brynhilda.

After a time, Gunnar, the king's son, heard of Brynhilda and wished her for his wife. Brynhilda had sworn to wed the man who rode though the wavering fire around her castle.

She swore this vow because she was sure no horse but Gran would go through the fire, and that Gran would not move unless Sigurd rode him.

Gunnar tried to ride through the fire, but his horse shrank back. He then mounted Gran, but Gran would not move a step. Then the queen gave a magic drink which made him look like Sigurd.

Disguised as Sigurd, Gunnar mounted Gran and the good horse plunged into the fire. The flames blazed up to the sky. But as Gunnar rode on, the flickering fire wall sank and soon he came to Brynhilda.

After three days, Gunnar, disguised as Sigurd took Andvare's golden ring and returned home, where the queen changed him into this own likeness again.

Then Brynhilda became Gunnar's wife because she had sworn to wed the man who would ride through the fire.

One day, Gudrun told Brynhilda that it was Sigurd who had ridden through the flames and not Gunnar. Brynhilda reproached Gunner until he threatened to have her chained.

She then opened the door of her bower wide and wept and wailed until Gudrun begged Sigurd to give her gold to quiet her.

When Sigurd went to the bower, Brynhilda lay upon a couch, and he remembered that it was he who had awakened her from her magic sleep.

When Sigurd remembered Brynhilda, he wished to take her and go away to her castle. But Gunnar had him killed while he slept. When Brynhilda saw Sigurd was dead, she killed herself with the same sword.

Gudrun mourned many years for Sigurd. At last her two brothers gave her a cup of magic drink and she forgot him and became the wife of

King Atli, the brother of Brynhilda.

Atli was angry because of Brynhilda's death. Besides, he wanted the gold which Gunnar had taken when Sigurd was killed. So he sent Gunnar an invitation to come to visit Gudrun.

Gudrun, knowing that Atli meant to kill her brother, sent him word not to come. But he never received the message.

When Gunnar came into Atli's palace, he saw many armed men. Atli said, "Give me the golden hoard which by right belongs to Gudrun." Gunnar refused, and Atli's knights sprang upon him and his men.

At last, only Gunnar and his brother were left alive. The brother was tortured to death, but he would not tell where the hoard was kept.

SIGURD THE VOLSUNG

Then Gunnar's hands were tied and he was cast into a den of serpents. Gudrun brought him a harp, and he played upon it so sweetly with his toes that all the serpents but one were charmed to sleep. This one, a great adder, crept upon him and stung him to death.

Gunnar had hidden the hoard in the Rhine and no man could find it. In revenge for the death of her kindred, Gudrun killed Atli and his two sons and burned the castle.

Thus, Andvare's words came true, and the gold brought only trouble to its possessor.

SPECIAL NOTE

YULETIDE WAS A FESTIVAL OBSERVED BY THE NORSE PEOPLE THOUGHT TO HONOR THE GOD ODIN AND THE WINTER SOLSTICE. IT IS STILL CELEBRATED BY MANY AS CHRISTMASTIDE (CHRISTMAS)

ODIN THE ALL FATHER

The great god Odin was the father of all the gods. He and his children dwelt in the city of Asgard at the end of the rainbow.

Odin's palace was as high as the sky and roofed with pure silver. In it was a throne of gold. When Odin sat upon the throne, he could see all over the world.

Each day, he sat upon the throne to see if everything was as it should be on the earth. He loved the people, the animals, and all the beautiful things of earth because they were the work of his hands.

Odin had two ravens which were as swift as thought. Every day, he sent the ravens to fly over the oceans and the land to see if any harm was being done. When they came back, they perched upon his shoulders and whispered in his ear all that they had seen.

Besides this there was a watchman who never slept. He was called Heimdal, the white god.

He stayed always at the foot of the rainbow, which was the bridge of the gods, to see that the frost giants did not come into Asgard and to listen to the sounds of Earth. So sharp were his ears that he could hear the grass and the wool on the sheep's backs growing.

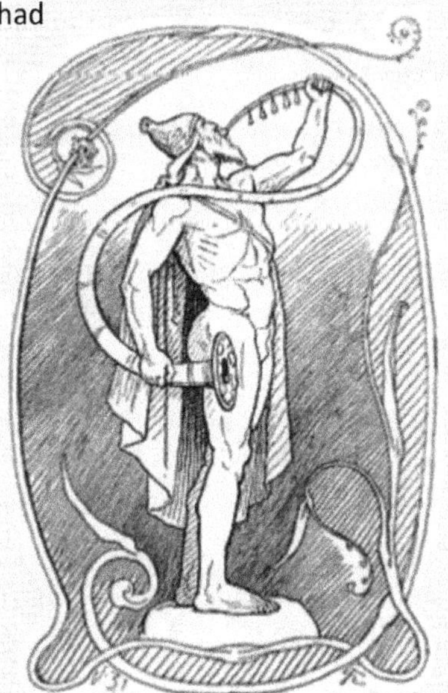

HEIMDAL THE WHITE

One day, when Odin mounted his throne, he saw that the earth was no longer green and beautiful. The air was full of snowflakes and the ground was as hard as iron. All was dark and cold.

The ravens, which had been sent out to see if all was well, came hurrying back to tell Odin that Hoder, the blind old god of darkness, had taken possession of the earth.

Heimdal, the watchman, called that he could no longer hear the music of the waterfalls and birds, and all the pleasant sounds of earth. Everything was mute with fear of the terrible god of darkness.

Odin called the gods together, and they looked with pity on the great Earth, which had been so pleasant a place.

Thor, the strong god, offered to go with his hammer and fight with the god of darkness, but Odin knew that Hoder could hide himself away from Thor. Then Balder the Beautiful, the god of light, whom all the gods loved, offered to go. So Odin gave him a winged horse, Sleipner, and he rode away across the rainbow bridge.

As soon as the light of Balder's shining eyes fell upon the poor, cold earth, it brightened and stirred. But the old, blind god Hoder brought all his forces of darkness to resist the god of light, and the earth lay as if dead.

Balder struck no blows as Thor, the strong god, wished to do. He did not even try to resist the god of darkness. He only smiled upon the earth and called to it to awake.

At last the blind god turned and fled before the light of Balder's face. Then the streams leaped up and sang, the birds came back and the flowers bloomed.

Everywhere the grass and the waving grain sprang up beneath Balder's footsteps, and the trees put out the gayest blossoms to greet him.

The squirrels and rabbits came out of the places where they had hidden themselves and danced and frisked with joy. Never before had the Earth been so beautiful.

But Hoder the blind god, in his realm of darkness, was only waiting for an opportunity to take possession of earth again. So Odin permitted Balder's mother to cross the rainbow bridge to help her son.

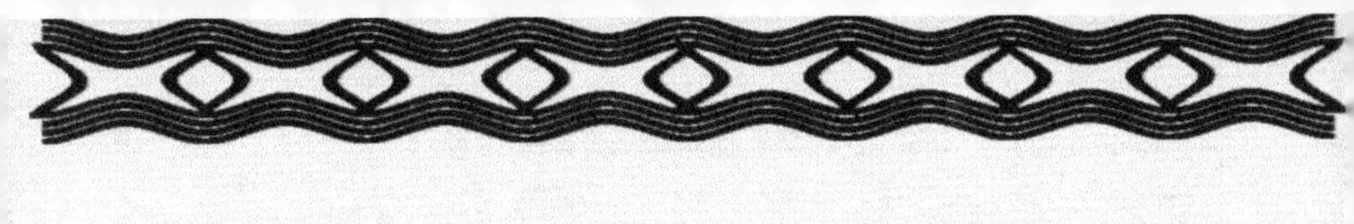

The goddess went through all the earth, begging each plant and stone and tree not to harm her son, who had brought them nothing but blessings. And every tree and shrub and tiny plant, and every rock and pebble, and every stream and little brook promised gladly. Only the mistletoe, which grows high up in the oak-tree and not upon the ground as other plants do, was forgotten.

Loke, who was a meddlesome god, always doing something wrong, found that the mistletoe had not given the promise, and told Hoder.

Hoder thought that because it was so little and weak, it could not really kill the god. So he shot an arrow tipped with a tiny twig of mistletoe at Balder. The arrow pierced through and through the beautiful god, and he fell dead. Then the earth put off her green robe and grew silent and dark for a time.

But because Balder the Beautiful had once lived on earth, Hoder could only make it cold half the year and dark half the day.

Even now, if you listen, in the winter you can hear the wind moan through the trees which fling their great arms in grief. And on summer mornings very early, you will find the stones and the grass wet with weeping in the darkness.

But when the sun shines, the tears are turned to diamonds and the earth is glad, remembering Balder the Good.

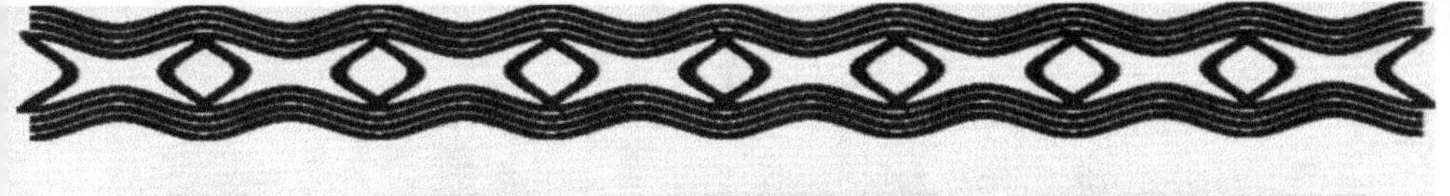

THE DEATH OF BALDER

I heard a voice, that cried,
"Balder the Beautiful
Is dead, is dead!"
And through the misty air
Passed like the mournful cry
Of sun ward-sailing cranes.

Balder the Beautiful,
God of the summer sun,
Fairest of all the Gods!
Light from his forehead beamed,
Runes were upon his tongue,
As on the warrior's sword.

All things in earth and air
Bound were by magic spell
Never to do him harm;
Even the plants and stones,
All save the mistletoe,
The sacred mistletoe!

Hoder, the blind old God,
Whose feet are shod with silence,
Pierced through that gentle breast
With his sharp spear by fraud
Made of mistletoe,
The accursed mistletoe!

- Henry Wadsworth Longfellow

LOKE

One day, Loke was wandering about idly, as he often did. He came near Thor's house, which had five hundred and forty rooms.

By the window sat Sif, Thor's wife, asleep. Loke thought it would be a good joke to cut off her beautiful hair and make Thor angry. So he crept in softly and cut off her hair close to her head without waking her.

When Thor came home and found out what had been done, he knew at once who had done it.

Rushing out, he overtook Loke, and threatened to crush him to atoms. To save his life, Loke swore to get the elves to make hair of gold for Sif that would grow like real hair.

Loke knew he had better do as he had promised, so he went deep down into the earth to Alfheim. When he came nearer, he looked through a crevice in the ground, and there were the elves at work. He could see them by the light of the forge fires.

Some were running about with aprons on and with sooty faces. Some were hammering iron, and others were smelting gold. Some were cutting out rock

crystals and staining them red for garnets and rubies. The elf women brought violets and the greenest grass to be found on the earth above. With these, they stained crystals blue and green for sapphires and emeralds.

Some of the elf women brought children's tears from the upper earth, and the gentlest elves changed them into pearls.

As fast as they were finished, the jewels were carried away by the little elf boys and hidden in the ground, where they are found to this day. If you wish to see what cunning workmen the elves were, look at the shining faces and straight edges of quartz crystals, or at the beautiful coloring of emeralds and rubies.

The little elf girls crept through the earth under the ocean and gave the pearls to the oysters to keep. Even now, the oysters shut their shells tight and will not give up the pearls.

Loke watched the little workmen a long time. Then, he went in and told them of his errand. Nothing delighted the elves so much as to have work to do. They promised Loke the golden hair, and at once began to make it.

A little elf ran with a handful of gold and an old grandmother spun it into hair. As she spun, she sang a magic song to give life to the gold. At the same time, the elf blacksmiths and goldsmiths set about making a present for Loke.

The blacksmiths made a spear that would never miss its mark. The goldsmiths made a ship that would sail without wind. Besides, it could be folded up and put into the owner's pocket.

Loke appeared before the gods with these wonderful things. To Odin he gave the spear, and to Frey the ship. Thor took the golden hair and put it upon Sif's head. Immediately it began to grow. At this, the gods pardoned Loke.

When Loke went out, he began to boast that the sons of Ivald, who

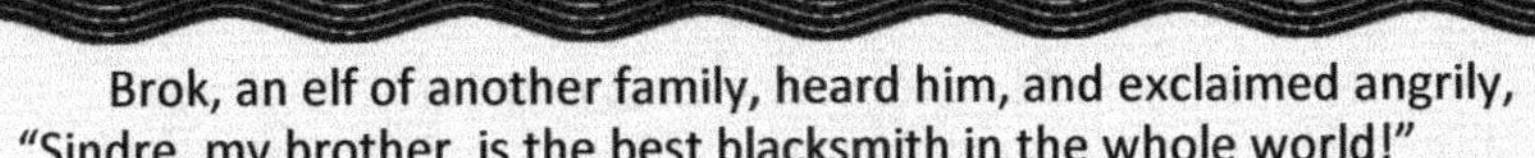

Brok, an elf of another family, heard him, and exclaimed angrily, "Sindre, my brother, is the best blacksmith in the whole world!"

Loke dared Brok to show him three gifts of Sindre's making equal to the spear, the ship, and the hair.

Brok hastened to Sindre and told him. The two brothers began the work at once. Sindre put a pig-skin into the furnace and told Brok to blow the fire with the bellows while he went out. Brok worked with a will. Loke had followed him, and now changed himself into a fly and stung Brok's ear. But Brok worked steadily, never stopping to brush it off.

Sindre came back and took out the pig-skin, and it had become a golden pig. So bright was it that it made the cave as light as day.

Then Sindre put a little piece of gold into the furnace and went out again. Again, as Brok worked at the bellows, the fly came, and stung him on the nose. But the elf did not stop for an instant.

When Sindre took out the gold it had become a magic golden ring. From it, every ninth night, dropped eight golden rings.

This time, Sindre brought a piece of iron and put it into the furnace. Brok began his work but Loke changed himself into a hornet and stung the elf on the forehead until blood ran into his eyes.

Brok bore it a long time. Then he paused a moment to drive away the hornet. Just then, his brother came in and said it was of no use to go on after he had once stopped.

Sindre took out the iron and it had become the mighty hammer Mjolner. But the handle was a little too short. This was because the elf had stopped when the hornet stung him.

Brok took the golden pig, the ring, and the hammer to Asgard and presented them to the gods. Thor had just lost his hammer in a great fight with the Midgard Serpent, so Mjolner was given to him.

This hammer could never be lost, because it would always return to the owner.

The pig, Golden Bristle, was given to the sun-god, Frey, because he has to take long journeys in dark places.

Odin kept the golden ring himself.

The gods voted Sindre a better blacksmith than the sons of Ivald. Brok demanded Loke's head, which had been wagered. The cunning Loke said he might have the head, but he must not touch the neck. So the elf did not get the head.

BROK AND SINDRE GET TO WORK

SPECIAL NOTE

THE TERM 'ELF' AND 'DWARF' WERE OFTEN USED TO DESCRIBE THE SAME TYPE OF PEOPLE IN NORSE MYTHOLOGY. THEY WERE ALSO KNOWN AS THE SVARTÁLFAR, OR 'BLACK ELVES'.

No god was allowed to sit on Odin's throne but Odin himself. One day, when Frey was alone in the palace, he sat upon the throne and looked over into Jotunheim.

There he saw a maiden come out of a low, dark house. As she walked down the pathway, the air became clearer and warmer. The earth brightened and grew green. When she went inside and shut the door, the light faded and the earth grew black again.

Around the low, dark house was a wavering wall of fire, and within the wall, fierce dogs kept watch night and day.

When the door was shut and Frey could no longer see the maiden, he went away sadly. He could neither eat nor sleep for longing to see her.

So sad was he that no one dared ask him his trouble. Skade, his mother, sent Skirner, his faithful friend, to find out what ailed him.

Frey told Skirner of the beautiful maiden and that he could never be happy unless she came to Asgard.

Then Skirner said if he could have Frey's horse and sword, he would ride through the flame wall, kill the watch-dogs, and bring Gerd to Asgard.

Frey gave his horse gladly. Skirner rode through the fire, although it roared in his ears and blazed far above his head.

When the dogs saw him, they set up a fierce howling, but Skirner quieted them with Frey's sword.

Gerd heard the noise outside and sent a servant to see what it was. The servant said an armed warrior stood at the door.

But Gerd knew he must be a god or he could not have passed the flame wall, so she bade the servant bring him in and give him food and drink.

As soon as Skirner saw Gerd, he took from his pocket eleven golden apples of the gods and offered them to her as a present from Frey.

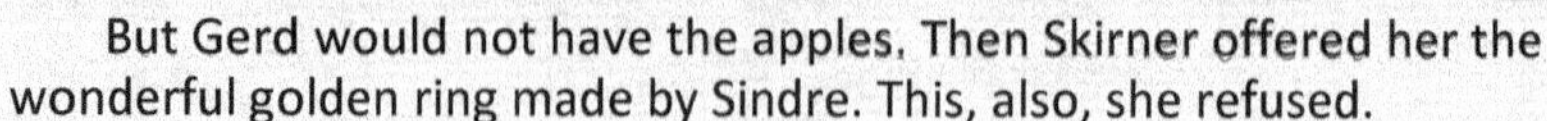

But Gerd would not have the apples. Then Skirner offered her the wonderful golden ring made by Sindre. This, also, she refused.

Then Skirner took out a magic wand and waved it over the maiden. As he waved the wand, he sang a magic song, telling of the warmth and light of Asgard and the beauty and gentleness of Frey.

As the maiden listened, she became enchanted with the glory of the city of the gods and no longer remembered her own cheerless land.

Then, Skirner took her behind him on Frey's horse and rode back across the rainbow bridge.

Frey stood by the gate watching. When he found that Skirner had not only brought Gerd, but that he had made her forget her home and love Asgard, he was so pleased that he let Skirner keep his sword.

Loke was a mischievous fellow. He was always getting the other gods into trouble. Sometimes they shut him up, but they always let him out because he was so cunning a threat he could help them to do things they could not do for themselves.

Once, he crossed the rainbow bridge to Jotunheim, the land of the giants, and brought home a giantess for his wife.

Very strange children Loke had. One of them was the Fenris-wolf. He was named Fenrer. All the gods knew he was a wolf as soon as they saw him.

But he went about among the children, playing with them like a good-natured dog. And the gods thought there was no harm in him.

Fenrer grew larger and larger, and the gods began to look at him with distrust. They feared he might some day grow too strong for them.

But Fenrer always looked good-natured and harmed no one. He did not even show that he had great strength, so the gods did not have the heart to kill him.

But they put it off too long. One day, they found Fenrer had grown so strong that it was almost too late to do anything with him.

All the gods worked day and night, until they had forged a chain they thought strong enough to bind the wolf.

Knowing they could not bind Fenrer against his will, all the gods came together for games. Thor crushed mountains with his hammer. The other gods showed their strength by lifting, leaping, and wrestling.

Then they brought out the chain and told Fenrer to let them bind him with it, so that he might show his strength by breaking it.

Fenrer knew that he could break the chain, so he allowed himself to be bound. He only drew in a deep breath and the chain dropped into pieces.

Then the gods forged a chain twice as strong as the first. Fenrer saw that his chain would be hard to break. But breaking the first chain had made him stronger, so he allowed this one to be put on him.

This, too, he broke, and the gods were in despair. They knew they could never make a stronger chain, and they feared the wolf more than ever.

Odin took his horse, Sleipner, and went on a seven days journey to the home of the dwarfs. They lived deep down in the Earth and had charge of the gold and diamonds and all other precious things. They were the most cunning of blacksmiths.

When Odin told the little people what he wanted, they all cried, "Never fear, Father Odin! We can make a chain that will bind the wolf."

When the chain was made, it was as light and delicate as a spider's web, but Odin knew it could never been broken.

As soon as Fenrer saw the chain, he was afraid of it. He knew if it were only a cobweb, they would never ask to put it on him. So he would not allow himself to be bound unless a god's hand was put in his mouth. At this, the gods only looked at one another. After a little time, Tyr, the bravest of all the gods, put his hand into the wolf's mouth.

The moment the chain touched Fenrer he knew he could never break it, and he bit off the god's hand.

But the Fenris-wolf was bound forever.

TYR THE BRAVE

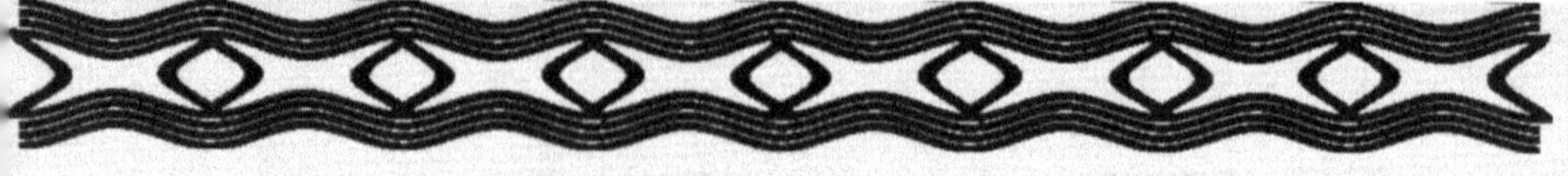

THE APPLES OF IDUN

Once, Odin and Loke were traveling together. They came to a field where a herd of black-horned oxen were grazing. They were very hungry, so they killed one of the oxen.

They tried in vain to cook the meat but it stayed raw in spite of the hottest fire they could make.

A huge eagle flew to a tree near them and called, "I will make the fire burn if you will share with me."

The gods were very glad to do anything that would give them food, so they promised to share with the eagle.

In a short time, the meat was cooked. The eagle flew down and laid hold of half of it.

Loke was angry and struck the eagle with a pole. To his surprise, the pole stuck fast and he could not let it go.

He was dragged over rocks and bushes until he begged for mercy.

Then the eagle changed into the renowned giant Thjasse. The giant said he would not let Loke go until he promised to deliver Idun and her apples into his hands.

Half dead with fright, Loke promised but he did not know how he could keep his promise.

Idun kept the apples in a strong box. Every day, she gave some of them to the gods.

When Loke returned, he told her he had seen much finer apples than hers just outside of Asgard.

Idun wished to compare her apples with those Loke had seen. So she took the box and went with him.

As soon as they were outside, Thjasse came in shape of an eagle. He carried Idun and her apples to Jotunheim.

Soon, the gods found themselves growing old and gray because they had no apples to eat.

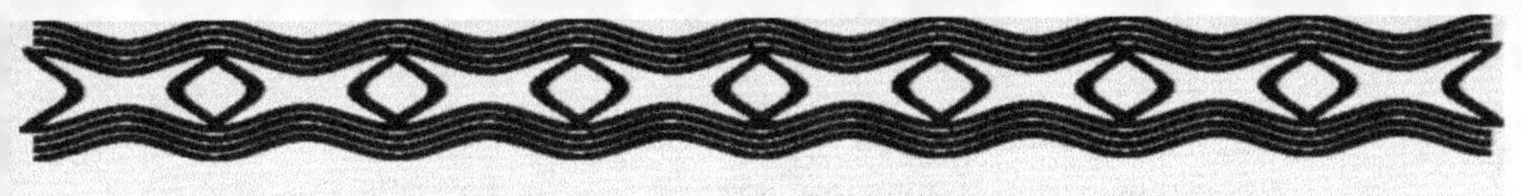

When they inquired, they found that Loke was at the bottom of the mischief as usual. The gods threatened to kill Loke if he did not bring back Idun and her apples.

Loke was frightened. He borrowed Freyja's falcon plumage and flew to Jotunheim.

Thjasse was out fishing. Loke changed Idun into a nut and flew back to Asgard with the nut between his claws.

Thjasse saw him and followed closely. The gods feared Loke would be overtaken, so they put chips on the walls of Asgard. The instant Loke was over, the set fire to the chips.

Thjasse could not stop in time, and his eagle plumage was burned. He fell down into the streets of the city and was slain by the gods.

THE BUILDING OF THE ASGARD FORT

The gods feared that the frost giants would invade Asgard while Thor was away fighting monsters.

Often, they spoke together of the danger. One day, Loke advised them to hire a workman whom he knew to build a fort strong enough to keep out the frost giants.

The gods listened to him, although they knew he seldom gave good advice.

The workman was brought into Asgard. Very strange wages he demanded. He said he would build the fort if they would give him Freyja, or the sun and moon, when it was finished.

The gods agreed to this, but they said he should have nothing if the fort were not finished by the first day of summer.

The workman said he would do the work if he could have Svadilfare, his horse, to draw the stones.

On the first day of winter they began the work, working night and day. At this, the gods were frightened. They feared the fort would be finished on the first day of summer. Sure enough, three days before the first day of summer, only one pillar was unfinished.

Seeing this, the gods threatened to kill Loke if he did not find a way out of the difficulty. They could not give Freyja and if the gave the sun and the moon, everything would be in darkness.

But on the last night, Loke changed himself into a monster and ran out of the woods before Svadilfare. The horse was so frightened that he ran away and the workman was forced to go after him. So the fort was not finished.

Seeing that he could not get his reward, the workman became a giant, as he really was, and Thor struck him dead with his hammer.

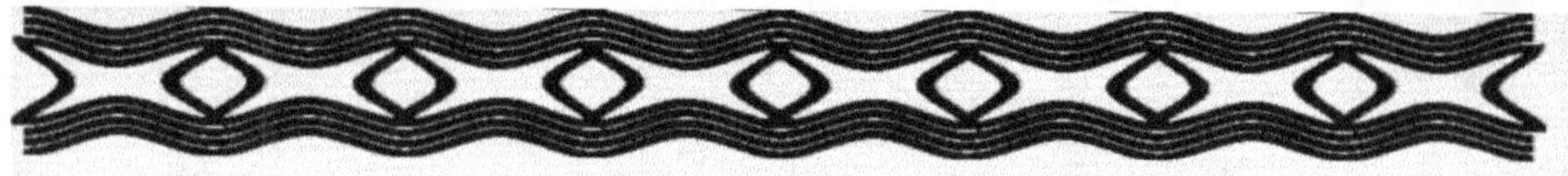

SVADILFARE IS FRIGHTENED BY LOKE

Thor was a strong god. So strong was he that he could crush mountains with one blow of his hammer.

His eyes shone like fire. When he drove in his chariot, the sound could be heard all over the earth. When he struck with his terrible hammer, fire streamed through the night sky.

On one hand he wore an iron glove to grasp the hammer and around his waist was a belt. Every time he tightened the belt, his strength was redoubled.

If he had crossed the rainbow bridge it would have fallen down. So every day he waded through four rivers to go to the council of the gods.

Thor was usually as good-natured as he was strong but sometimes he had sudden attacks of anger. Then he drove furiously in his chariot, pointing in every direction with his hammer. Sometimes he did damage which, with all his strength, he could never repair.

Very often, Thor did kind things. Once, the dwarf, Orvandal, did not go into his home in the ground when the frost giants where in the land. They caught him and took him to Jotunheim.

Thor waded across the ice-cold river Elivagar to the land of the giants and brought Orvandal back in a basket. When they were nearly across, Orvandal put one toe outside and it was bitten off by the frost giants.

Thor liked nothing better than to go on long journeys, seeking adventures.

Once he set out in his chariot drawn by goats. Loke the Cunning went with him.

Night came. Thor made himself no larger than a man and asked to stay all night in a poor man's hut by the seashore.

The man welcomed them. Thor killed his goats, and the poor man's wife cooked them.

When nothing was left but the bones, Thor told the children to put them all into the skins on the floor. But one of the boys broke a bone to get the marrow.

At dawn the next day, Thor touched the bones with his hammer, and the goats sprang up alive. But one of them was lame. When the family saw the bones changed into living goats, they were very much frightened.

Thor was angry because the goat was lame and grasped his hammer so tightly that his knuckles grew white. At first he meant to kill the whole family, but after he thought, he only took away two of the children for servants.

They crossed the ocean that day and found a forest on the other side.

When it grew dark, they went into a cave to sleep. In the cave, there were five small rooms and one large one. All night they heard a great rumbling noise.

Early in the morning when they went out, they found an immense giant sleeping on the ground. The noise they had heard was the giant's breathing, and the cave was his glove.

When Thor saw him, he tightened his belt of strength and grasped his hammer. But just then the giant awoke and stood up. His great height so amazed Thor that he forgot to strike and only asked the giant's name.

The giant replied that he was Skrymer. Then he asked to go along with Thor. Thor said he might, and they all sat upon the ground to eat **58** breakfast.

E. BOYD SMITH

After breakfast, the giant put Thor's provision sack into his own and carried both. All that day he strode in front and Thor followed.

At night, they stopped. The giant drank a small brook dry and at once lay down on the ground and fell asleep.

Thor found that he could not untie the sack. At this, he was very angry.

He tightened his belt and went out where the giant lay. He swung his hammer above his head and struck the giant's forehead with all his strength.

The giant awoke and rubbed his eyes. Then he said sleepily, "I think a leaf must have fallen upon me." With that, he fell asleep again.

Thor and the others lay down without any food, and the giant snored so loud that they could not sleep.

Again Thor arose. He tightened his belt twice and struck the giant with a harder blow than the first. The giant only stirred and muttered, "This must be an oak-tree, for an acorn has fallen upon my forehead."

Thor hurried away and waited until the giant once more slept soundly. Then he went softly and struck him so hard that the hammer sank into his head.

This time, the giant sat up and looked around him. Seeing Thor, he said, "I think there are squirrels in this tree. See, a nutshell has fallen and scratched my forehead."

"But make ready to go now. We are near the palace of Utgard."

"You see how large I am. In Utgard's palace I am thought small. If you go there, do not boast of your strength."

With that, he directed Thor to the palace, and went away northward.

At noon, they saw a palace so high that they had to bend back their heads to see the top of it.

The gate was locked. So they crept in through the bars and went from room to room until they came to the hall where sat Utgard with his men around him.

For some time he pretended not to see Thor. Then with a loud laugh he said, "Ho! Ho! Who is this little creature?" Without waiting for a reply he cried, "Why, I believe it is Thor of whom we have heard."

Then speaking to Thor for the first time, he said, "Well, little man, what can you do? No one is allowed here unless he can do something."

Loke, who was quicker then Thor, said, "I can eat faster than anyone here."

Then Utgard said, "Truly that is something. We will see if you have spoken the truth."

The giants brought in a trough filled with meat. Utgard called Loge, one of his men, to contend with Loke.

Loke and Loge met at the middle of the trough. But Loke had only eaten the meat, while Loge had eaten meat, bones, and trough. So Loke was beaten.

Then Utgard asked what Thjalfe, the boy Thor had taken from the seashore, could do. Thjalfe replied that he could outrun any man there.

Utgard called a little fellow whose name was Huge. Huge so far outran Thjalfe that he turned back and met him half-way.

Utgard said, "You are the best runner that ever came here, but you must run more swiftly to outrun Huge."

Then Thor was asked in what he wished to contend. He answered, "In drinking."

Utgard sent the cup-bearer to bring his great drinking-horn.

When Thor took the horn in his hand, Utgard said, "Most of the men here empty it at one draught. Some empty it at two draughts. But no one ever takes three."Thor put the horn to his lips and drank deep and long. When he was out of breath, he lowered the horn. To his surprise, very little of the water had gone.

Utgard said, "I should have thought Thor could drink more at a draught."

Thor did not reply, but drank again as long as he had any breath. This time enough was gone so that the horn could be carried easily without spilling any of the water.

Utgard said, "Have you not left too much for the third draught?"

Thor became angry. He put the horn to his lips and drank until his head swam, his ears rang, and fire floated before his eyes.

But the horn was not nearly empty, and he would not try again.

Then Utgard said, "Will you try something else?" Thor replied that he would. Utgard said, "We have a little game here that the younger children play.

The young men think nothing of lifting my cat. I would not propose it to you if you had not failed in drinking."

The cat ran in, and Thor did his best. But he could only lift one paw from the ground.

Then he called for someone to wrestle with him, but Utgard said the men would think it beneath them to wrestle with Thor. Then he called his old nurse, Elli, to wrestle with him.

The tighter Thor gripped the old woman, the firmer she stood. Soon he was thrown on one knee and Utgard sent the old woman away.

The next morning at dawn, Thor and Loke and the two children prepared to go away.

Utgard gave them breakfast and went a little way with them.

When he was ready to go back, he asked Thor how he liked his visit. Thor replied that he had done himself dishonor.

At this Utgard said, "I will tell you the truth now that we are out of my palace. You shall never come into it again. If you had known your strength, you should not have come this time.

"In the forest, it was I you met. If I had not half a mountain between your hammer and my head, you would have killed me. There is the mountain. The three waves you see were make by the three blows of your hammer.

"One end of the drinking-horn stood in the sea. When you come to the shore, you will see how much water is gone.

"What you took for the cat was the great Midgard Serpent which encircles the earth and holds its tail in its mouth. The nurse was old age. No one can resist her."

Hearing this, Thor readied his hammer to strike. But Utgard and the palace vanished and left only a grassy plain.

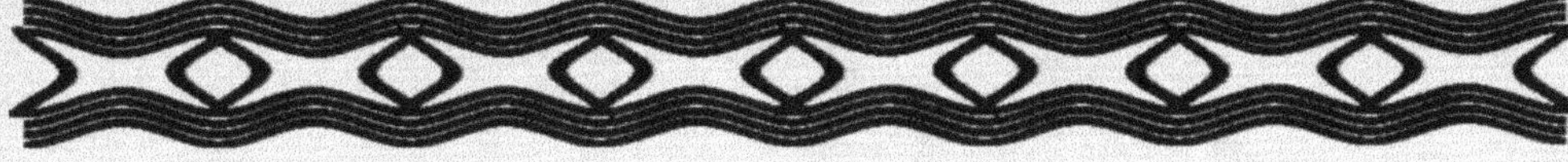

Here amid icebergs

Rule I the nations;

This is my hammer,

Mjolner the mighty;

Giants and sorcerers

Cannot withstand it!

These are the gauntlets

Wherewith I wield it,

And hurl it afar off;

This is my girdle;

Whenever I brace it,

Strength is
redoubled!

The light thou beholdest

Stream through the heavens

In flashes of crimson,

Is but my red beard

Blown by the night-wind,

Affrighting the nations!

Jove is my brother;

Mine eyes are the lightning;

The wheels of my chariot

Roll in the thunder,

The blows of my
hammer

Ring in the
earthquake!

- Henry
Wadsworth
Longfellow

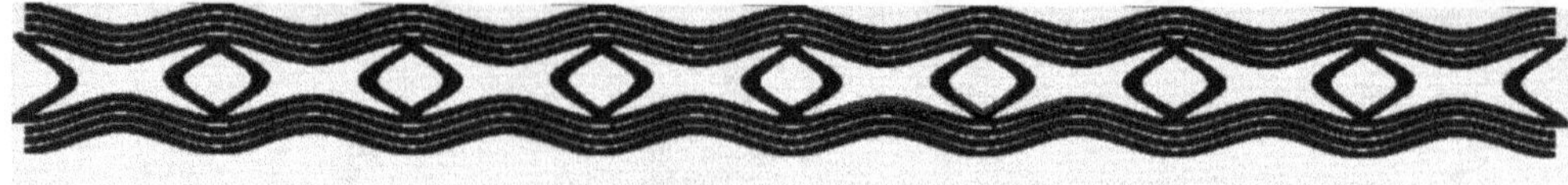

THOR AND HYMER

Far down in the cool depths of the ocean dwelt Aeger, the sea-god, in his shining palace.

The water lapped softly against its clear green walls. All the herds of Ran, the sea-god's wife, played about it.

Within sat Aeger on his throne, and the winds and waves, which were his children, went abroad to do his will.

On a day when the ocean lay calm and quiet in the sunlight, the gods feasted in Aeger's palace.

But Aeger's great kettle was lost, and there was no meat for the guests.

Thor shook his great hammer in anger and vowed to bring back the kettle. But no one could tell him where to find it.

Tyr said, "Just within the borders of Jotunheim lives Hymer. He has a kettle a mile deep. But he who goes for it must be wary, for Hymer is a dog-wise and dangerous giant."

Thor cried, "I fear no giant! Show me the way and I will bring the kettle!"

So the two gods passed out of Aeger's sea-green hall and away through groves of coral. Dolphins and sword-fish played beside their pathway without fear.

Soon the gods reached the upper world. There, they made themselves look like two young men. Then they traveled away to the land of snow.

On the icy shore of the ocean, they found Hymer's house. At the door they were met by Hymer's beautiful wife, who was Tyr's mother.

The house was dark and gloomy. Very glad was Tyr's mother to see the guests. She bade them welcome, but told them to hide under the kettles.

Hymer came home late, his beard shining with frost. The beams of
 the low, dark house shook under his feet.

"My son is here," said his wife when he had shaken the frost from his hair.

"Where is he?" said Hymer.

"Behind the post," replied his wife. Hymer's eyes blazed. He stared hard at the post. Instantly it flew into splinters. Eight of the kettles fell clanging to the ground. Out sprang the gods and faced the giant.

When Hymer saw his old enemy, Thor, he was frightened. So he bade them welcome, and ordered three oxen to be roasted whole for supper.

Thor ate two himself, and Hymer thought he would kill no more of his fine black oxen. He thought he would have fish for the next meal.

At dawn the next day, Thor saw Hymer getting his boat out. Thor dressed quickly and asked to go along to do the rowing.

Hymer said, "You might take cold if you stay out as long as I stay, and the rowing might tire you."

Thor was angry enough to box the giant's ears. But he only answered that he could row as far as Hymer wanted to go, and that Hymer would be the first to want to come back.

Thor then asked Hymer for some bait. But Hymer said if he wanted to fish he must find his own bait. At this, Thor marched up to the finest ox in Hymer's herd and wrung its head off.

Thor rowed with such strength that Hymer was surprised. When he wanted to stop, Thor said they were not out far enough yet.

Then Hymer cried in fear, "If we go any farther, we will be in danger from the Midgard Serpent." At last, Thor stopped, and Hymer soon caught two whales.

Thor took out a line he had brought from Asgard and baited the hook with the ox's head.

The moment the bait dropped to the bottom of the ocean, the Midgard Serpent swallowed it. Then Thor tightened his belt of strength and pulled till his feet were through the boat and he stood on the bottom of the ocean.

The Serpent's head rose to the top of the water. When Hymer saw it, he turned pale and trembled with fright. Just as Thor drew back his hammer to strike, Hymer cut the line and the serpent sank to the bottom.

Thor gave the giant a blow with his fist that nearly ended his life.

Taking the two whales into the boat, Thor rowed to shore. There, he took up the whales and the boat and carried them all into the house at once.

At supper, the giant challenged Thor to break his goblet by throwing it. Thor threw it against the walls and upon the floor, but it would not break.

Then the giant's wife whispered, "Throw it against Hymer's forehead." Thor did so, and the goblet shattered.

Then the giant said Thor might have the kettle if he could carry it away.

Thor tried to lift it, but could not at first. As he tried, he grew stronger, and, at last, he put the kettle over his head. But it reached down to his heels, and the handle tripped him.

Thor and Tyr traveled as fast as they could with the kettle. After they had gone a long way, Tyr saw Hymer and a host of his friends rushing after them.

Thor put down the kettle and killed all the giants.

Every harvest time, Aeger made a feast for the gods in memory of Thor's bravery.

THOR'S FIGHT WITH HRUNGNER

One day when Odin was riding abroad on Sleipner, he passed by Jotunheim.

There he met Hrungner, one of the giants. Hrungner said, "Who are you and where did you get that fine horse?"

Odin replied, "I will wager my head that there is not so good a horse in Jotunheim."

Hrungner answered angrily that his horse, Goldmane, could take longer strides.

Then Odin challenged Hrungner to a race. In a short time, Goldmane was brought and the race began. Sleipner was always ahead.

Hrungner thought of nothing but of overtaking him. Before he knew it, he had followed Odin into Asgard.

The gods were feasting and they invited the giant to eat with them. Thor's drinking-horn was brought and Hrungner empted it at a draught.

By and by he began to boast of his strength. "I will tear down Asgard, kill the gods, and carry off Freyja," he cried, crashing Thor's drinking-horn upon the table.

But the sound made by the drinking-horn called Thor, who was far away.

Soon, a muttering as of distant thunder was heard. Flashes of fire streamed through the air and there was Thor with his hammer in his hand.

"Why is this giant allowed to feast with the gods?" Thor demanded. "He should never have been allowed to enter Asgard."

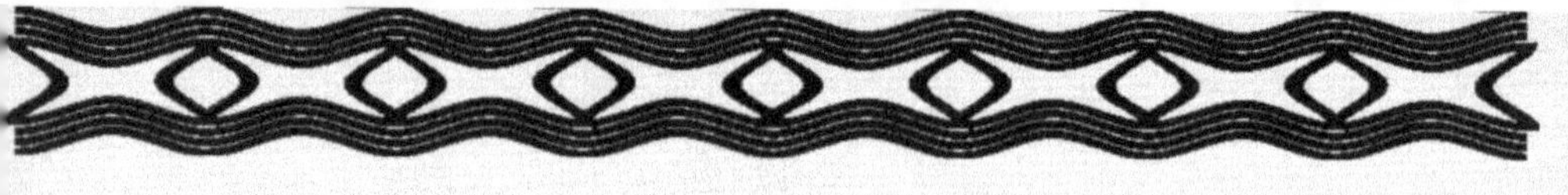

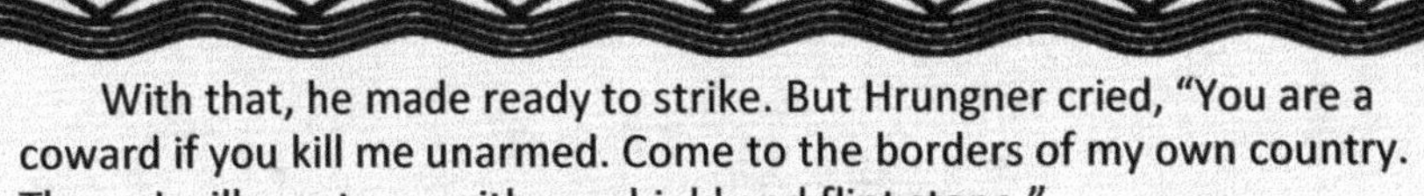

With that, he made ready to strike. But Hrungner cried, "You are a coward if you kill me unarmed. Come to the borders of my own country. There, I will meet you with my shield and flint stone."

So a day was appointed and Hrungner went back to Jotunheim. There, he made a huge clay giant, nine miles high and three miles across the shoulders. He put a horse's heart into the giant because that was the largest heart he could find.

On the appointed day, Thor appeared in his chariot, fire flashing from his eyes, mountains trembling down as he passed, and hurling his hammer before him.

His servant, Thjalfe the swift runner, went before and told Hrungner that Thor could attack from under the ground as well as from the air. So Hrungner put his shield under is feet. As Thor approached, so frightened was the clay giant that his horse's heart fluttered within him and perspiration flowed off him in streams.

Hrungner hurled his flint stone, and Thor his hammer at the same moment. They met in the air and the flint stone was broken into two pieces.

One piece fell to the earth and became a mountain while the other piece struck Thor's head and he fell upon the ground.

The hammer struck Hrungner and he fell dead with his foot on Thor's neck. Thor could not remove the giant's foot. All of the gods tried, but none of them could lift it.

Then Thor's son, a baby three days old, came and lifted the foot with one hand saying, "Sorry am I that I did not meet the giant, for I think I could have killed him with my fist."

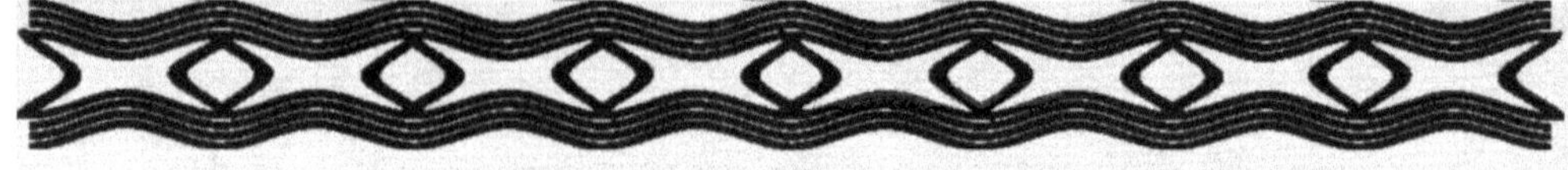

THOR AND THRYM

When Thor was away on one of his journeys, he laid his hammer down for a moment, and went away without it.

The giant Thrym found the hammer and he carried it to Jotunheim, burying it eight miles deep.

When Thor missed his hammer, he went back and found that it was gone. He knew that no one but a giant could have lifted it.

Back he drove to Asgard, still in such a rage that the gods themselves trembled. But they trembled more when they heard Thor's story. They feared that the giants could no longer be kept out of Asgard.

Loke borrowed Freyja's falcon plumage and flow to Jotunheim. The first giant he met was Thrym. "Why have you come to Jotunheim?" said the giant. "I have come for Thor's hammer," replied Loke. "Ho! Ho! Ho!" laughed the giant, "the hammer is buried eight miles deep. I will give it to no one until he brings me Freyja for a wife."

Loke flew swiftly back to Asgard, and told Thor what the giant had said.

Thor thought of nothing but his precious hammer. He rushed to Freyja and told her to make ready to go to Jotunheim.

At this, Freyja was so angry that Thor, big as he was, trembled and left without saying anything more.

Loke said, "We will dress you up like a woman, and what a beautiful bride you will be."

So Thor had Freyja's dress put on him, a necklace around his great throat, and a veil over his face. But even then, his eyes blazed like fire.

Loke dressed himself like a maid and they went to Jotunheim in Thor's chariot.

When Thrym saw them coming, he had a great feast prepared.

Thor ate a whole ox and ten salmon. Thrym's eyes stood out with surprise. But Loke whispered, "Freyja longed so much to come to Jotunheim that she has not eaten nothing for seven days."

At this Thrym was so pleased that he leaned over to look her face. But he stared back when he saw the blazing eyes. Loke said softly, "Freyja longed so much to come to Jotunheim that she has not slept for seven night."

When the feast was over, Thrym brought the hammer and laid it in Freyja's lap.

The moment Thor's fingers touched the handle, he sprang up, tore the veil from his eyes, and drew back the hammer to strike.

So angry was he that he laid the giant dead with one blow.

Thor and Loke went away, leaving nothing but a heap of blazing sticks where the house had been.

THOR AND GEIRROD

Once, Loke put on Freya's falcon plumage and flew away to Jotunheim. As he flew about amusing himself, he came to the home of the giant Geirrod.

Here he perched on the roof and looked in through an opening.

Geirrod saw the bird and sent a servant to catch him but the wall was high and slippery. Loke laughed to see how much trouble the servant had climbing up.

He thought he would fly away when the servant had almost reached him but when he tried to fly away, his feet were held fast. So he was caught and taken to Geirrod.

As soon as Geirrod looked into the falcon's eyes he knew he was not a bird. The giant asked Loke many questions, but Loke would not answer a word.

Geirrod locked him in a chest for three months without food.

At last, Loke confessed who he was. To save his life, he promised to get Thor to go to Geirrod's house without his hammer and belt.

Loke went at once to Thor and told him Geirrod wanted to fight him.

Thor's eyes began to flash fire, and he rushed to his house for his hammer and belt. But Loke had been there before him and hidden them.

Thor was so angry that he would not wait to find them. Away he went in his chariot to fight the giant.

On the way, he met a giantess who told him Geirrod was a dog-wise and dangerous giant.

She gave Thor her gloves, her staff and her belt of strength.

Soon, Thor reached a wide river. He put on his belt of strength and plunged into the water.

When he reached the middle of the river, the waves went over his shoulders.

Thor looked up and saw that Geirrod's daughter was making the waves with her hand so he threw a stone and drove her away.

Then, he reached the bank and caught a branch and drew himself out of the water.

When Thor reached Geirrod's house, he was given a room by himself. There was only one chair in the room.

Thor sat in the chair. Suddenly, it was lifted to the roof. He raised his staff and pressed against the roof with all his strength.

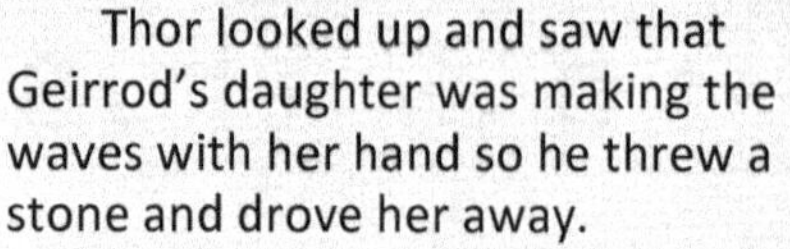

The chair fell to the floor. Two of Geirrod's daughters had been sitting under it.

Soon, Geirrod sent a servant to invite Thor to come and see games.

Great fires burned all down the hall. When Thor came near Geirrod, the giant seized a piece of iron and threw it at Thor.

Thor caught it in his iron gloves and raised his arm to throw it at Geirrod.

Geirrod ran behind a post. Thor hurled the iron. It went through the post and through Geirrod, and through the wall into the ground outside.

Thor took the gloves and staff and belt back to the giantess.

He never went anywhere without his hammer again.

THE SONG MEAD

Once there lived on Earth a poet who sang songs so beautiful that all created things were charmed by them.

Two hill trolls who hated the poet because he was noble and good invited him to their home underground and there killed him.

They caught his blood in two cups and mixed it with honey to make mead. If any man drank the mead, it would make him a poet, too. But the trolls hid it in a dark place and would give it to no one.

One day, the trolls enticed a giant into a boat with them and drowned him. When his wife came to inquire about him, they sent her down the sea-shore. Then they threw a rock from the cliff and killed her.

Suttung, the son of the giant, came to see what had become of his father and mother. He threatened to kill the trolls.

To save their lives, they gave him the precious song mead. Suttung took it home and put it into his cellar. His daughter, Gunlad, guarded it night and day.

Odin wished to drink the mead, so he made a journey to Jotunheim.

There he saw nine thralls mowing in a field. He offered to whet their scythes. When they found what a keen edge the scythes had, they wanted to buy the whetstone.

Odin threw it up and said that whoever caught it might keep it. In trying to catch the whetstone, the nine thralls killed one another with their scythes.

Then Odin went to the master of the thralls and asked for work. The giant hired Odin because he was so much in need of workmen.

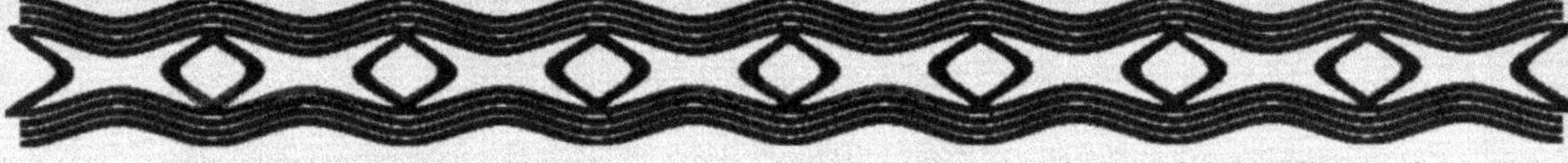

This giant, whose name was Bauge, was Suttung's brother. Odin said he would work all summer for one draught of the song mead.

Bauge told Odin to begin the work and he would see about the mead. When he found that Bolverk, as Odin called himself, could do the work of the nine thralls, he wished to keep him. But Suttung would not give one drop of the mead.

One day when he was away, Bauge and Odin went to his house. They took with them an auger that Odin had brought from Asgard.

Odin bade Bauge bore a hole through the wall of the cellar. Bauge pretended to have bored through. But when Odin blew into the hole, the chips flew into his face.

Bauge bored again. This time, the chips flew the other way. Then Odin changed himself into a worm and crept through. Before Gunlad knew he was there, he had drunk every drop of the mead.

After drinking the mead, Odin, with all his power could not remain a worm. He changed at once to a beautiful bird, and flew away. When he reached Asgard, he sang such songs as the gods had never heard.

GEIRROD

Once, two children, the sons of a giant, strayed into Asgard. They were too young to know the way back to their home.

Odin and Frigg, his wife, adopted the two boys and called them their sons. Odin cared more about Geirrod, but Frigg loved Aganor, the younger one, best.

When they were grown, Odin gave each of them a kingdom in his own realm. Aganor left his kingdom and went back Jotunheim.

Odin was pleased more than ever with Geirrod because he did not follow his brother, but Frigg heard it said that Geirrod only appeared to be good, and that he tortured strangers to make them give up their gold.

When Odin heard this, he decided to go to see Geirrod and prove that it was not true. So he made himself look like a very old man, and went to Geirrod's house. Instead of giving him a seat at the table and bed, Geirrod chained him between two fires.

For eight days the old man was silent, although no food was given to him. He had not even any water but for once when Aganor, Geirrod's son, ran in and gave him a cupful.

At last, the fire became so hot that it burned the old man's clothing.

Then, suddenly, he began to sing a wonderful song in a deep and musical voice. Geirrod knew at once that it was Odin.

In his despair, he slew himself with his sword. The little Aganor who had pitied the stranger became king in his place.

LOKE'S PUNISHMENT

After the death of Balder, the gods sent Hermod, his brother, to the realm of the dead to beg the goddess of death to release him.

Hermod rode nine days and nine nights through valleys so dark that he could see nothing. At last, he came to a bridge made of glittering gold.

Modgud, the maiden who kept the bridge, stopped him and said, "What is your name?" Hermod told his name, but did not say he was a god.

Then the maiden said, "Why do you, who are living, try and cross this bridge? You shake it more than a whole army of dead men."

Hermod replied, "I come to seek Balder the Beautiful, and I pray you let me pass quickly, for the gods wait wearily in Asgard." When the maiden saw that he was a god, she hindered him no longer.

Hermod rode on until he came to the kingdom of the dead. Spurring his horse, he leaped over the gates without touching them.

He rode swiftly to the palace and entered. There, he saw Balder in the highest seat and spent the night with him.

The next morning he begged the goddess of death to release Balder and told her of the sorrow of the gods and the despair of the earth.

The goddess replied, "If all created things, the lifeless as well as the living, will weep for Balder, I will release him. But if anything refuses to weep, he shall not return to Asgard."

Hermod rode back to the gods, who sent messengers throughout all the world to beg everything to weep for Balder. All things, men, animals, plants, and even stones wept willingly, and the messengers returned gladly because they thought Balder would be released.

But on the way to Asgard, they found a giantess who said, "Balder never brought me gladness. I will not weep. Let Death keep him."

So because there was one thing that would not weep, Balder remained in the realm of death and the gods were forever grieved.

This giantess was Loke, but the gods did not know it until long afterwards. When they found it out, they decided to punish him. Loke fled to the mountains. There, he built a square house with four doors so he could see in every direction. He would often change himself into a salmon and hide in a nearby stream but Odin sat upon his throne and saw Loke's hiding place.

One day, Loke wove a net like the one he had once borrowed from Ran, the sea-god's wife. Just as it was finished, he looked out and saw the gods coming. He threw the net into the fire and plunged into the stream.

But the gods saw the shape of the net in the ashes and wove one like it. When it was finished, they held it by the ends and dragged it through the water.

Loke hid between two stones and the net passed over him. The gods felt that something living had touched the net, and the next time, they weighted it so heavily that Loke could not slip under it.

This time, he leaped over the net. The gods tried again and Thor waded in the middle of the stream. As Loke tried to leap over, Thor caught him. He was so slippery that he almost slid through Thor's hands, but Thor grasped his tail tightly and he could not escape.

Loke was then bound so that he could never loose himself, but his wife was allowed to bring him food and water. So he was punished for his many evil deeds.

VOCABULARY

Ae-ger

Alfheim

Andvā-re

Balder

Baw-ge

Be-le

Bōlverk

Brage

Bryn-hilda

Idun—Ēdun

Ivald—Ēvald

Cl-le

Frey—Fray

Freyja—Fray-a

Frithiof—Freet-yof

Geīr-rod

Gni-ta

Hel-ge

Ho-der

Hrŭng-ner

Hu-ge

Hy-mer

Jotunheim—Yo-tun-heīm

Kriēm-hild

Lo-ke

Lo-ge

Mjol-ner—Meŏlner

Magn-e

Nibelung—Nē-bē-lōōng

Sleīpner

Skā-de

Svād-il-fa-re

Skry-mer

Strōmkarl

Thōr

Thōrsten

Thjasse—Te-as-se

Thjalfe—Te-al-fe

Thrym

Val-hal-la

Frut—Frōōt

Gudrun—Gōōd-rōōn

Hetel—Hātěl

Hartmut—Hart-mōōt

Hegelings—Ha-gē-lings

Her-wig—Hār-wig

Horant—Hō-rant

Ortweīn

Sigeband—Sē-gē-bänd

Sturmland—Stoorm-länd

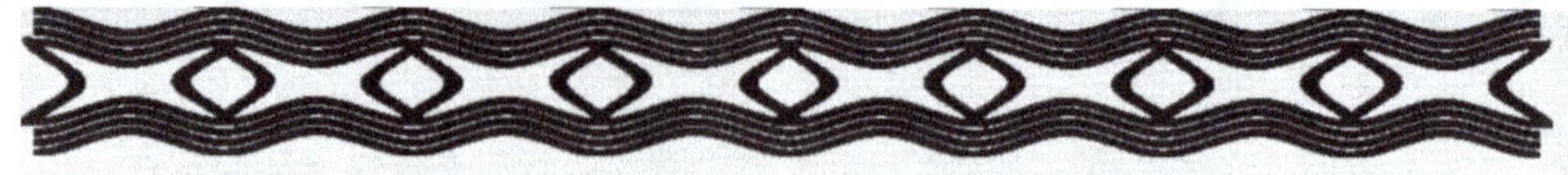

We would like to thank everyone who made
this publication possible up to and including:

B. A. Gabrielle & Christine Almstrom

www.ingramcontent.com/pod-product-compliance
Lightning Source LLC
Chambersburg PA
CBHW070316120726
47910CB00007B/2513